Just a Cowboy's Convenient Marriage

Flyboys of Sweet Briar Ranch in North Dakota
Book One
Jessie Gussman

Published By: Jessie Gussman

Contents

Acknowledgments   V

1. Chapter 1   1

2. Chapter 2   9

3. Chapter 3   15

4. Chapter 4   27

5. Chapter 5   36

6. Chapter 6   47

7. Chapter 7   52

8. Chapter 8   62

9. Chapter 9   70

10. Chapter 10   78

11. Chapter 11   85

12. Chapter 12   92

13. Chapter 13   102

14. Chapter 14   105

15. Chapter 15   114

16. Chapter 16   123

17. Chapter 17   132

18. Chapter 18   139

19. Chapter 19   150

20. Chapter 20   158

21. Chapter 21   167

22. Chapter 22   178

23. Chapter 23   183

24. Chapter 24   193

25. Chapter 25   199

26. Chapter 26   201

27. Chapter 27   205

Just a Cowboy's Best Friend   212

A Gift from Jessie   223

Escape to more faith-filled romance series by Jessie   224
Gussman!

Acknowledgments

Cover art by Julia Gussman
Editing by Heather Hayden
Narration by Jay Dyess
Author Services by CE Author Assistant

Listen to a FREE professionally performed and produced audio-book version of this title on Youtube. Search for "Say With Jay" to browse all available FREE Dyess/Gussman audiobooks.

Chapter 1

Was that a pig?

Smith Long looked out from under the brim of his cowboy hat.

Yup. It was definitely a pig waddling up the sidewalk of...he racked his brain. What was the name of this rinky-dink town in North Dakota again? His aunt had lived here all her life, but it was barely a dot on the map.

Sweet Water. That was it.

He looked again. Yup, it was a pig.

Its hind end swung back and forth as it made its way up the sidewalk.

It was early May, but at least the sidewalk was clear, the snow melted away for the winter.

He remembered various times over the years visiting his aunt where there had been snow on the sidewalk in May.

Even at a young age, he remembered thinking who in the world would want to live in a town that had snow in May?

Someone who had lost everything and had nowhere else to go. *That's you.*

Slapping his leg, he adjusted the brim of his hat and stepped around his pickup.

He couldn't resist one last glance at the pig before he stepped up on the curb, right in front of Patty's Diner.

The new community center—new to him, although it had been built for a decade or so—was around here somewhere, and his great-aunt April would be there with her crafting group. They had a funny name for themselves, but he couldn't remember that either.

He supposed he spent a lot of his life focused on himself and not really paying attention to the people around him. That was why he couldn't remember the name of the town or the name of the crafting group, and it could possibly be part of the reason why his wife had left him.

It wasn't the reason he had lost everything, though.

Maybe his mind drifted a little, thinking about the things he'd done, and the decisions he made, and the one that still haunted him. He believed someone who had said they believed in him, and he trusted them far more than he should have.

His line of thinking was brought up short, though, as what he would have sworn was a woolly mammoth—but he was pretty sure they were extinct, so it couldn't have been—went flying by him. The tip of its horn just grazed his T-shirt right over his abs. If he'd been wearing a winter jacket, it would have hooked him.

It was going full speed ahead after the pig.

He sighed. Small towns. They always had those quirky things, didn't they?

Not that he'd spent much time in them. After being in the military, he settled in Raleigh, a nice, warm southern city, and started his own business.

More aware of his surroundings, he took his eyes from the cow and looked back from whence it had come. Perhaps there was something else that was just waiting to run him over.

He was glad he had looked. A woman, long brown hair streaming out behind her in curly waves, her face set in determined lines, her arms pumping as her feet slapped the sidewalk, raced forward, every line of her body straining to go faster.

Smith almost grunted. This woman had a lot to answer for. He could have been killed by the horn that had—he looked down at his T-shirt to confirm his suspicion—poked a hole in his attire.

"Excuse me," he said, his drawl a little more pronounced, as it always was when he forced the politeness that had been stamped into him from birth. It always came out when he was hiding his emotions.

At the same time he spoke, he stepped into the woman's path.

She took another three steps before she realized he wasn't moving. She screeched to a halt, her arms flailing, her face lifting, moving from a determined frown to an annoyed grimace.

"Excuse me. I need to catch that cow."

"Your cow almost caught me." He pointed a finger at his T-shirt. Maybe the people of Sweet Water needed to catch up with the twentieth century, where people didn't allow their animals to roam freely on the sidewalks and think that it was perfectly okay.

He knew someone who was new in town probably shouldn't ride in on the first day expecting to change everything, but this could be, quite literally, a matter of life and death.

The woman looked at his T-shirt, the annoyance not leaving her face as she squinted. He thought, but couldn't prove it, of course, that she might have been exaggerating her squint.

"I'm sorry. I need a magnifying glass to see whatever it is you're pointing at."

Smith managed to keep his lips from twitching. He liked a woman with a little spirit. Not that he was interested in a woman. "Nice. Sweet Water has entered the glass age, at long last."

Maybe that date thing was a little bit mean, a little hit to all the small towns that always had so much trouble leaving the past behind, and he must have poked this woman right where she was sensitive, because her lips tightened even more, and her back straightened like someone had jammed a rod down her backbone.

"You can make fun of small towns all you want. There was no glass age."

"I'm sorry. You are correct. But there was definitely an age when people decided it was a bad idea to allow their animals to run all over town, and they kept them fenced in. Sweet Water hasn't gotten to that age yet, apparently." He raised his brows, annoyed that she hadn't seemed to care about the tear in his T-shirt and the fact that someone could have gotten seriously hurt because of her animal running wild on the streets.

"Spoken like someone who's never owned an animal in his life before. If you had, you'd know that occasionally, despite your best intentions, they do get loose."

"Maybe you should have something more solid in your business plan than best intentions."

Best intentions were worthless without actual actions to back them up. And an ironclad, signed contract. He knew that from experience.

"You must make friends everywhere you go with your honeyed words and happy compliments." The woman looked like she was going to roll her eyes but stopped herself just in time.

Back in the day, he was always happy. A bit of a goof-off even. He had a lot of fun with his buddies in the Air Force. He'd been serious when he needed to be, but he'd been able to cut loose with the best of them.

But life had shown him that most of the time, the universe was conspiring against him, and if the universe wasn't, the opposite gender was. He couldn't really remember any woman ever being a faithful friend without an ulterior motive.

Not even his mother.

Certainly not this woman, who thought she owned the entire town and could allow her animals to run wild.

"I'm not trying to make friends with everyone. I'm just trying to keep people safe. To keep them from being gored by runaway bulls charging through town."

"He's not a bull; he's a steer."

"Whatever. He put this hole in my shirt. Another couple of inches, and I'd be picking my intestines up off the ground."

"I suppose at that point, you'd still find the energy to lecture me, even if I offered to help you," the woman muttered.

"I wouldn't want you to help me. You'd probably walk off with them."

"I can promise you, I'm not after your intestines."

"I wasn't sure whether Sweet Water was in the selling body parts business or not."

The woman's lips flattened. "Black hearts aren't going for anything."

"I figured you'd know the market value of them if anyone would."

"You don't even know me!" The woman stomped her foot on the sidewalk but couldn't go around him without brushing him since he was doing a rather effective job of blocking the entire way.

He wasn't sure why he was giving her such a hard time. Maybe he was getting mean. He hoped not.

But if she had been through what he had, she would be too. Plus, he really did have a hole in his T-shirt.

"Are you going to let me by?" She dropped her arms and acted like she was preparing to walk forward to his right.

He moved a little. To his right. "You owe me a T-shirt."

"What? That's ridiculous!"

"How is it ridiculous for you to replace what your animal destroyed?"

"First of all, your T-shirt is not destroyed. It's barely broken in. And second, how do I know that the hole wasn't there to begin with?"

"First of all, you said it yourself, my T-shirt is barely broken in. It wouldn't have a hole. Not unless I was almost gored by a runaway, crazy bovine. Second, I don't lie."

"It's been my experience that if someone has to state the fact that they don't lie, they do."

That comment almost brought him up short. After all, it was true.

If someone had to say they weren't a liar, they probably were. That had been his experience too. But he was deep enough in this argument that he wasn't going to concede any ground.

After all, winning the argument was more important than being right, or something like that.

Smith decided his best bet was to pivot. "This is no way to welcome people to your town. Have your animals almost gore them to death and then stand and argue with them about whether or not they have the right to be on the sidewalk."

"I didn't say anything about you being able to be on the side-walk." The woman put her hands on her hips. Her eyes flashed, and her cheeks were red. If Smith hadn't taken such an instant dislike to her, there would be something very appealing about her.

Maybe he was just deluding himself, since he'd decided that all women were the same, because there absolutely was something very appealing about this woman.

"You seemed to insinuate that it was my fault when I'm the one that has a hole in my T-shirt."

"It's not your fault." The woman's brows drew down a bit, like she was trying to make sure she didn't fall into some trap he was setting for her.

"Then, you agree, it's yours."

"I didn't say any such thing."

They had moved so that they were almost nose to nose. Well, as nose to nose as two people whose height difference was at least eight inches could be.

She didn't let him intimidate her, which he admired, but it also challenged him in a way that he could hardly resist. It made him want to win the argument.

"I just want you to admit that your animals shouldn't have been running around loose. That they need to be penned up. And if you can't handle them, you should give them to someone who can, in order not to endanger the lives of the citizens of this town, visitors, and the animals themselves."

"And I said that you're talking like someone from the city who's never owned an animal in his life before." She ground her teeth and shook her head, as though she couldn't believe she was even still arguing about it. He felt like they had come full circle as well.

She spoke. "Would you please move out of my way? I need to try to catch my cow." She narrowed her eyes. "Before he puts a hole in someone else's T-shirt."

"Gladly." He managed not to add that if he never saw her again, it would be too soon. But he didn't really mean that. Even though he wanted to say it for some reason.

After all, he knew that the odds of him meeting the one woman who was different than all the other women he'd ever known were vastly against him. Not to mention, this woman seemed odd, the kind of crazy lady every small town had at least one of.

The last thing he needed was to get involved with a woman like that.

He stepped to the left.

She moved to the left at the exact same time.

He moved to the right quickly.

So did she.

"Aaargh! Would you please let me by!" She stomped her foot, not that it made any difference whatsoever, other than to probably send a zing up her leg. She actually looked cute, but he managed not to laugh.

"You stand right there. I'm going to move." He waited until her eyes met his, which he probably shouldn't have done. A small zap of what felt like electrical current flew down his back and made his fingers tingle. He told himself it was because of their argument and not because of any kind of attraction between them.

He was very much over acting like a fool because of any kind of attraction he might feel.

She crossed her arms over her chest, and some part of him, some sneaky, tiny, juvenile part of him wanted to stand right where he was, waiting until she moved before he did, but he shoved that part of him back and stepped slowly aside.

"Thank you," she spat out, not sounding the slightest bit grateful, as she dropped her arms, took two cautious steps to get by him, then started running again.

He knew, because he turned to look. Maybe he shouldn't have, but he couldn't seem to help himself.

He grinned and shook his head at her, or maybe himself, he wasn't sure. He didn't have the time or the money to get involved with a woman, but he had to admit she was the most interesting one he'd met in a very long time.

Deliberately pulling his eyes away, he turned back toward Patty's Diner, opening the door and stepping inside as the bell above him jingled.

Chapter 2

S mith walked into Patty's Diner.

His buddies, Gideon and Jonah, had gone in with two more of their good friends from the Air Force and bought Sweet Briar Ranch just north of town.

He hadn't gone in with them because his Aunt April had promised him she would deed over the ranch she had grown up on. It was apparently not in great condition, so it wasn't a huge gift, but she had some stipulations she had said they would need to discuss.

He didn't care what her stipulations were. Basically, he would have a home with no upfront money necessary, and that's exactly what he needed right now, since he had no money.

He shoved that thought aside as well because it just made him angry. He should have money, and plenty of it, but he'd been double-crossed and swindled.

Gideon and Jonah were supposed to meet him at the diner, and he looked around as he stepped in, seeing that it was mostly empty.

A pretty, young-looking woman bustled behind the counter in the window at the back.

His buddies had told him that the diner had recently changed hands. They mentioned it just in passing as a point of interest, like they might have been considering going into the food service business themselves.

They might as well. They knew as much about running a diner as they did about running a ranch.

All of them had spent time in the Air Force, which was hardly great preparation for making a living in rural America.

"Smith!" Jonah said, standing up out of the corner booth where he was sitting, facing Gideon.

His greeting made Gideon turn around. A smile broke over his face, and he stood as well.

They might be odd-looking friends. They probably wouldn't be friends at all, but they'd been assigned to the same crew in the Air Force and had survived a hostage situation together.

That type of thing had a tendency to bond fellows together, and it had done that to six of them. Gideon and Jonah, and the two men they had bought the ranch with, Baker and Zeke. Then there was Eli, their commander who had, if Smith had heard correctly, recently been dishonorably discharged.

That had shocked Smith to his very toes, because he had never known a man more honest and upright than Eli.

"We were starting to think you weren't going to make it." Jonah held out his hand, and Smith shook it before shaking Gideon's, and they all sat back down.

"I said I'd be here."

"I know, and we could see you out there on the sidewalk tussling with that cute girl. You always were a ladies' man."

"Was. Those days are long past. I don't care if I never see another woman." He looked around quickly to make sure he hadn't offended anyone with that statement. But there were no women in sight. Even the young lady in the back didn't have the right angle to be able to see through the window to their table.

Gideon and Jonah were quiet at his statement. They knew a little of what had happened. The bare bones. Not the details, and certainly not the feelings of anger and frustrated rage that he fought with for what felt like a long time but had just been months.

"Did you ever get any resolution out of that?" Jonah asked softly.

"No. She got away with everything. I could probably get a lawyer to dig even deeper, but the fact of the matter is, I trusted her, and our agreements were mostly verbal. Stupidity on my part, and a good lesson, I suppose." For sure. From now on, everything, every single thing that he ever did was going to be written down and notarized if necessary. There was no way he was going to trust a woman to keep her word. Not ever again.

"Well, don't hate us, but there's a wedding going on today, and the entire town is invited."

"The entire town?" Smith looked up, his brows furrowed.

"Yep. I guess that's what they do around here. I don't even know the groom, but I know one of his friends, Gus, who invited us to go. Said everyone was going to be there. Got a little huffy when I said I didn't think we'd make it."

"Let me get this straight. A friend of the groom who happens to be someone you know invited you to go to the wedding of a man whom you've never met, and he got upset when you said you didn't think you were going to go?"

Jonah shrugged and blew on his coffee. "Apparently that's the way small towns are. Everybody's supposed to be there, and you're supposed to bring food if you have any. If not, you just bring whatever you have."

"I sure hope you're not bringing food. If you are, I'm definitely not going."

"I'm bringing food, just none that I made myself. I stopped at the store and grabbed a few bags of chips and some dip."

"And I'm bringing my horse to give horse rides for the kids." Gideon added his bit even though Smith hadn't asked.

"You have a horse?" That was news to Smith. And potato chips? Jonah was bringing potato chips to a wedding?

"Sure. I got a cute little mare that was called bombproof. Apparently, bombproof means that they're gentle enough that if a bomb goes off beside them, they're not going to run off with you. Gus said that would be the perfect horse to give rides to the kids at the wedding, and since I didn't have anything else to bring, I figured I might as well."

"So you're bringing a horse to the wedding. And you're bringing potato chips?" He looked across the table at Jonah before looking at Gideon and then back again.

"Yep," they said at the same time. Both of their eyes were twinkling, so Smith figured maybe he was missing the joke.

"So...what's the punchline?" he finally asked. He couldn't figure it out.

"No punchline. Apparently Tadgh and his girlfriend Ashley are tying the knot, the whole town is invited, and everybody is supposed to bring something."

"Even if you don't know either of the couple."

"That's right."

"And everyone will be offended if you don't go. Or someone will be. Small towns are weird that way. And trust me, as soon as you parked in front of Patty's Diner, the underground message system that's faster than the Internet around here—" At that statement, Jonah snorted, but Gideon ignored him and kept on going. "—made sure that everyone in town knew someone new had arrived. Now they know that you're talking to us, and they will definitely know if you don't go to the wedding. People will be offended."

"Right." He held his hands out. "If they know I'm new in town, they ought to know that I don't have anything to bring to the wedding, and therefore I can't go."

"That's not a good enough excuse. I tried that one when I was talking with Gus. That's why I ended up at the store buying potato chips. I got some extras, so that can be what you bring too."

Smith wanted to argue more. After all, he had things he had to do. But if it was true that everyone in town was going to be at the wedding, he wouldn't be able to talk to Aunt April until after the wedding anyway. Plus, if this was going to be his new hometown, he didn't want to offend anyone. The woman he just ran into was right. He was a little surly, a little grumpy, a little mean.

He didn't mean to be that way, but life had just shaped him, and what was he to do about it?

You can choose how you want to act. How you respond. Whether you allow the events of your life to make you bitter or better.

He didn't like hearing that. Because, so far, he'd chosen to allow them to make him bitter.

He didn't want to think about that. Because he really didn't want to be better. He liked being surly and mean. He liked having people give him a wide berth and respect him. It made him feel like he wouldn't have someone taking advantage of him again, the way Kylie had.

Still, he didn't want to be off-putting or make enemies on his first day in town. Plus, he might be able to talk to Aunt April at the wedding and go straight out to the ranch when he was done.

"What time is it all going down?" He figured they'd go out to their new ranch, they could show him around a bit, and they'd come on back in this afternoon.

Jonah looked at his watch. "Starts in about five minutes or so. Gus said these things never start on time, and people all mosey in at all hours."

"It starts in five minutes?"

As he said that, the woman who had been working behind the window came out, drying her hands on her apron. "You guys don't have to settle up right now, just lay your money on the counter before you go, and lock the door behind you. I'm heading out to the wedding."

And just like that, she put the towel over a rack behind the counter, walked around it, and strode out the door.

"I don't think you were kidding," Smith said as he stared after the retreating back of the woman. She was joined by two girls who must have been playing beside the diner. Smith didn't watch them but turned back to his buddies.

"We told you. Things are a little different around here."

"It's gonna take a little bit to get used to it, but they're mostly good changes." Gideon grinned that devil-may-care grin that Smith had come to see as trademark Gideon.

Smith thought about the crazy woman chasing the cow and pig down the street.

He supposed his friends were probably right. Living in a small town, on a ranch, was going to be a lot different than living in a city.

He had a feeling there were some things he would never get used to.

Chapter 3

Abrielle looked around the community center, her heart happy.

Sweet Water was home to not quite a thousand people, and she bet every single one of them was here today. Plus, a few people from surrounding areas and Rockerton, a larger town south of Sweet Water.

It wasn't that Tadgh and Ashley were so popular or even well-known. Tadgh was from Ireland and Ashley was new to the area, although she'd spent more than a year in Sweet Water a decade ago.

It was just that small towns loved celebrations, and what was a better celebration than a wedding?

Abrielle loved them herself, even if she most likely would never have one of her own. If she did, this was the kind she wanted though. Not one with all sorts of flash and jazz, but one that felt warm and welcoming and like the couple was putting on a celebration, not to make themselves look good or feel good but to make their friends feel welcome and included and to celebrate with no pressure on a day that was special to them.

To her, a wedding was like throwing a party to celebrate a person's marriage. It was less about everything being perfect and more about everyone having a good time.

"Isn't Ashley beautiful?" Teagan asked, her elbow on the table, her hand holding her chin as she stared dreamily at the bride.

"All brides are beautiful," Piper, her sister, answered.

Abrielle nodded, not needing to say anything as Piper and Teagan talked about brides and dresses and weddings, the way they had been for a while, and Abrielle allowed the conversation to flow around her.

Piper and Teagan and their other two sisters lived close to her—they were her closest neighbors on the ranch she was...borrowing.

When she had lost her job in Rockerton two years ago and couldn't make the rent on her apartment, Teagan, who had gone to school with her, had told her about the ranch beside them where no one was living.

Of course, Teagan had offered for Abrielle to live with them, but somehow it seemed a little less intrusive for her to squat on a ranch that wasn't hers than for her to move in with four sisters who were already crowded.

So, she'd checked with the lady who owned it, and since the ranch was in such disrepair and had been unoccupied for a long time, she had allowed Abrielle to live there in exchange for Abrielle paying the electric bill and the taxes and taking care of any repairs the place needed.

While there had been a lot of repairs—and a lot more still needed—she did have the opportunity to do what she had always wanted to do, and that was to plant a big garden and take her produce to the farmers market, selling it there, along with some crafts she made on the side.

"Abrielle's going to be next," Zaylee said, stirring Abrielle from her contemplation.

"Next for what?" she asked easily. She was usually pretty bubbly and happy. Always with a positive outlook. But maybe it was her run-in with that surly man on the sidewalk, or maybe it was the wedding, the happiness of the couple, and the feeling that it would never be her, but she seemed to be questioning her choices in life.

Here she was, almost thirty, living in a house that wasn't hers and working hard for the first time in her life to do something that she'd always dreamed of. Maybe she should be further along in her life. More successful, with a nice house and a two-car garage, 2.3 children, and a husband who adored her.

None of those things were in her foreseeable future.

"Next to get married, of course," Zaylee said, like it was the most obvious thing in the world.

"The four of you are unmarried, and two of you are older than I am. Why me?" she asked, smiling to let them know that she was fine with it. If God wanted to drop a man in her lap, she'd marry him. As long as he wasn't a jerk.

She thought again of the man on the sidewalk. Like that man. There was no way she would marry a man who didn't have laugh lines. Who looked like he spent more time grumbling and complaining than he did looking to make people happy. She wanted a man who smiled and made jokes—clean jokes. Who didn't get upset over every little thing. Who was easy to talk to. Friendly.

"Because you know men are intimidated by us. There are four of us, and we always seem to be together since it takes all four of us to run that ranch." Teagan laughed, looking around at her sisters.

They all nodded, and Abrielle had to agree. It was kind of intimidating to see the four of them together. And they had such a great bond. They had taken her under their wing themselves, or she might have been too intimidated to try to get to know them.

None of the sisters were so desperate to get married that they were willing to do anything about it. They were working too hard to keep the ranch afloat.

In North Dakota, that wasn't an easy thing. If it wasn't the weather that was working against a person, there were diseases or market volatility or some kind of issue with their animals.

The sisters had seen it all.

Abrielle had heard about it. Although she hadn't experienced it. She'd grown up in the town of Sweet Water, with her parents owning the barbershop. She was familiar with ranchers but not with actual ranch life and the work it took.

She wasn't overly interested in it, either. She loved the vegetables she grew and the dried herbs and crafts. That's always where her heart had been.

"You pick him, I'll marry him." Maybe she shouldn't have said that, but that's the way she felt. She didn't really want to take the time to date and get to know someone, and decide whether or not they were compatible, figure out they weren't, and then move on finding someone else. Just the idea seemed exhausting.

She'd done that a lot in her twenties, but she wasn't interested anymore. Finding a mate was too much work. And too little return for the effort. Plus, she had been wrong more than once thinking that a man was a great catch, only to find out he was selfish and self-centered and out to use her.

"Really?" Teagan said, and she sounded intrigued.

Abrielle shrugged her shoulders. "Why not? I mean, I want someone with integrity. Someone who's going to keep his word. Someone who has a history of being honest and faithful. I don't want a jerk."

Right there, that nixed about ninety percent of the male population. In Abrielle's opinion anyway.

"All right. Fair enough. I think we can probably trust God to find you a man that's not going to be a jerk." Teagan looked around at her sisters. They nodded.

Abrielle didn't like the look that was on their faces. "God and chance are two different things."

"If God orchestrates everything, then He's involved in every chance."

"Yes, but that doesn't mean that it's His perfect will."

"And chance is the best we're going to get today. They're about to toss the bouquet, and you need to be there to catch it."

"All four of you are unmarried as well."

"And none of us said that we wish that God would drop a man into our lap so that we wouldn't have to go after him," Waverley said very reasonably. Waverley, as the oldest of the sisters, often was the most reasonable.

As Abrielle watched, Ashley stood up from the head table and carried her bouquet to the front while Miss April, the unofficial wedding coordinator, called out to the congregated people that Ashley would be throwing her bouquet. She called all unmarried women over the age of eighteen to the front.

Abrielle looked around, not wanting to be the first person to walk out.

Unfortunately, her classmates—the people who would be the same age as her—had done what she had done, and that was, once they graduated, they moved out of town.

There really weren't any young unmarried women in Sweet Water.

Not many.

As she looked around, it felt like there was only one. Her.

She gave a pleading glance to her friends. "Guys. I don't want to walk up there by myself."

"You can't expect God to drop a man in your lap if you're not willing to walk twenty feet to the front of the room to catch one, okay? Come on. You can't expect to not have to do a little bit of something."

"It's not that I really want—"

"Just go," Teagan said, giving her shoulder a shove.

Awkward silence had fallen around the room. It felt off, after having such a happy, fun celebration.

Ashley stood at the front of the room, obviously not enjoying her role as the sole person in front of everyone.

"Anyone?" she asked, and her voice sounded a little shaky.

Her husband, normally jovial and smiling, had a worried expression on his face and looked like he was about to move from where he stood, holding the garter. Abrielle hadn't even been paying attention and didn't know when he had taken that off.

"I'm coming!" she called out, hopping up from her chair, the main focus of her attention on Ashley and trying to make her feel less conspicuous and awkward.

Ashley had been kind to her. Her career was in marketing, and she had given Abrielle a few tips and helpful contacts where she might be able to sell more of her produce.

She couldn't just repay that kindness with an unwillingness to participate in her wedding.

She hurried to the front, where Ashley smiled, looking relieved, and handed her the bouquet.

"Thank you," she said as she took it. "It's beautiful, by the way."

"Thanks. I think you'll be glad you came up. Tadgh has already chosen the man who's going to get the garter. His friends were teasing him that he didn't have anything to bring to the wedding, so in order to make him feel better, Tadgh told him that he could just participate in the garter ceremony. So there is no drama with who puts the garter on."

Abrielle nodded, having never thought that the garter was dramatic anyway. Usually it was the ladies that were scrambling for the bouquet.

Sometimes they didn't even throw a garter. It seemed to be a little outdated. After all, who wore garters?

But it was a fun wedding thing, and she supposed that it didn't hurt to participate, even if it was strictly for the enjoyment and entertainment of the guests.

But as Abrielle stood there, she slowly became aware that the man who was walking toward her, holding a garter in his hand, was the same man, in the same T-shirt, with the same miniscule hole, that had confronted her on the sidewalk in front of Patty's Diner.

Sometimes it felt like the good Lord used her life for His own entertainment. She didn't know how else to explain this.

There were a thousand people in this room. That man could not be the only unmarried male, and she was certainly not the only unmarried female. And yet, here they were.

As he drew closer, the high school band, who was providing music for the occasion, started playing some kind of romantic melody as Miss April said, "I don't think we need to tell you guys what to do. Here's your chair." She pointed to a chair that Abrielle hadn't noticed up until that point, too horrified to look anywhere other than the man, who walked toward her.

He looked equally horrified.

"You," the man said, sounding like he spit out the word like it was poison in his mouth.

She wasn't sure she could allow him to touch her. The idea made her skin crawl.

Okay. Mostly it made her skin crawl. The guy was a grouch and a jerk. It didn't matter that he filled out his T-shirt quite nicely or that she suspected if he smiled he would be extremely handsome.

"Is this your idea of a joke?" she asked, looking at the chair and then at the man and realizing she had no idea of what they were supposed to do. Other than he was supposed to put the garter on her leg. Was she supposed to sit down in the chair? She'd seen it done several different ways.

"I thought it was yours," the man mumbled, looking around and then seeming to become resigned.

"A nightmare maybe. Definitely not a joke. Certainly not one I would deign to play on myself."

"The joke's on me," the man said, looking again at the chair.

"I think not. You're the one who accosted me on the sidewalk."

"I accosted you? This is what your animal did to me." The man pointed at the hole, if that's what a person could call it, in his T-shirt. It wasn't that big. Maybe pinhead size. And it probably wasn't made by the horn of a cow.

But she couldn't prove it, because she couldn't see it. She highly suspected the man was lying. Probably wanting her to buy him a new T-shirt. And if she had any money at all, that's what she would have done instead of arguing with him on the sidewalk. But she couldn't afford to lose the argument, because she couldn't afford to compensate him in any way for anything.

Although, she would have figured something out if her animal truly had hurt his property.

Probably.

Plus, she had been supposed to bring Billy, the town's Highlander steer, to the wedding so that kids could pet him afterward. But she hadn't been able to catch him and didn't have any idea where he was.

Technically, Billy wasn't really hers. She'd just adopted him. He was used to hanging out around Sweet Water, almost like the town mascot. He'd been doing it all winter, and the townsfolk had thought it was funny, but Abrielle was the one who had started feeding him on a regular basis.

The pig, she had no idea about. Other than Billy had seemed to have fallen in love with it.

"Did you ever catch your runaway attack machine?" the man asked as he gave the chair one more glance, then walked over and sat down in it.

With him sitting in the chair, she wasn't sure exactly what that left for her to do. So she ignored the fact that he had moved at all and said, "No. I wasn't able to go after it, because someone detained me. And by the time I was able to leave," she gave him a dirty look, "my cow was nowhere in sight."

She didn't want to explain how the cow wasn't really hers or any of the other stuff. The guy seemed to twist everything she said into something that she didn't mean or that was somehow ridiculously dumb.

He didn't make her feel that way, surprisingly, though. She actually felt invigorated when they talked, like the way a person felt when they had met an equal match at checkers or chess.

"You never got your cow? So it's still roaming freely on the streets of Sweet Water?" The man sounded aghast.

"I couldn't show up to the wedding in jeans, so I had to go change. I had a limited amount of time to look for him, and I couldn't find him." She still was loath to tell him that the cow wasn't exactly hers. After all, she had been chasing Billy pretty hard. Billy had been running from her. Not because he was scared. He had been running after the pig.

She was guessing that the pig was a lot like Billy. It just showed up, and the town of Sweet Water would take it in and make it their own.

"Are you going to do this or what?" the man asked, lower because the music had gotten softer. It seemed like no one was talking and everyone's attention was focused solely on them. She supposed they had been making a show, too, glaring at each other and snapping. Even if people couldn't hear their words, it was obvious by their body language that they weren't happy with each other.

"I'm not sure. You're sitting in the chair." She pursed her lips. "I thought that I was supposed to sit in the chair."

"Oh."

She wasn't sure, but she thought maybe under his naturally dark complexion his cheeks were reddening. "Haven't you done this before?"

"I never paid attention. I've been to a few weddings, but I've never been roped into this before."

"Me either. Usually people are fighting over the bouquet. But not today. It's almost like they were conspiring to get me up here."

"I felt the same way. But it couldn't be true, since I just rolled into town today."

"You wouldn't believe what small towns can do." She said that under her breath as they exchanged places, and she sat down on the chair.

"Since we've established that I'm the ignorant one, this is supposed to go up your leg, right?"

"Yeah. You can stop at my knee. No need to embarrass both of us any more than what we already have."

"No argument from me on that one."

The way he said it made her feel like it was going to be a hardship for him to even touch her at all. She tried to pretend that didn't hurt, but she was lying. Because it did. Even if she didn't like him—actually, she totally disliked him and wasn't attracted to him at all. Well, not much.

Whatever. She hated examining her feelings, because they were always so complicated. It was easier to just tell herself how to feel and then hope that her emotions got in line.

She adjusted herself in her chair, and he went down on one knee. The crowd clapped and hollered, but the man wasn't much of a ham, because he slipped the garter over her foot as fast as he could, yanked it up her leg, and put it right on her knee.

"There. Got that over with."

She knew he probably didn't mean it as an insult, but it felt that way.

"Hey, you two. Here's your dance," someone called out.

The music changed, and the man blinked and looked around.

"We have to dance?" The question sounded like someone had just told him he had to cut off his left foot and feed it to crocodiles and he was asking if he really had to.

She hadn't realized there was a dance either. The wedding couple had already danced, then Ashley had danced with her father. Tadgh's parents hadn't made it over from Ireland for the wedding, which was part of the reason the town had made sure to go all out. He had lived there long enough that everyone felt like he was one of their own, and when his family couldn't be there, everyone stepped in.

There was a lot of cheering, some catcalls, and a bunch of encouragement that was starting to grow awkward as she sat there, not wanting to get up and spend even more time with this man who seemed to insult her every time he opened his mouth.

She hated that, because she kinda thought that she might not have too much trouble liking him.

If she could get over her dislike of him.

And that's why feelings were complicated because both statements were true.

He held his hand out. "Come on. The sooner we get started, the sooner this nightmare will be over."

Another insult.

"Forget it. I don't want to make you spend one more second with me than what you have to. You've done enough." She stood, looking him in the eye, with a challenge in her own, before she lifted her chin and announced to the entire crowd, "There will be no dance. This man has suffered through my presence long enough."

Maybe that was a little dramatic, but she wasn't used to feeling unhappy. Usually she could, and did, put a positive spin on everything.

But his insufferable attitude and his every word that came out of his mouth making it seem like he could barely stand to be around her, coupled with their altercation on the sidewalk, made everything be too much.

She knew she should say something nice to him, some kind of farewell that would make sure he understood that if they saw each other on the street again they could greet each other without wanting to look the other way or ignore the person. But she couldn't.

It was all she could do to keep from crying as she walked quickly back to the table where Teagan and her sisters sat.

She didn't know what happened at the front of the room, didn't know what the man was doing, and honestly, or mostly honestly, she really didn't care.

Chapter 4

"**I**t was awfully kind of you to stay and help clean up, Smith," Aunt April said as Smith threw the last bag of garbage into the dumpster.

He had had no idea that Aunt April would be the last person to leave the wedding.

Dark had descended a long time ago, and the petting zoo that had been set up outside for the children, as well as the area where they had been able to ride horses and even a llama, had been abandoned an hour ago.

The woman who had embarrassed him in front of everyone had found her cow, because he'd seen her outside holding it with a halter and lead rope, with a lot of happy children sticking their hands into its shaggy fur. The cow seemed to be enjoying all the attention, although, it might be Smith's imagination, but he thought there might be a longing in its eye for the pig it had been chasing.

Regardless, after what the woman had done to him, walking away from him in front of the entire town, he hadn't had any time for her and turned away from the sight.

He had been right. She was just like every other woman he'd ever met. Her concern was solely for herself and what she could get out of him, not caring how she used or abused him.

Or embarrassed him.

He had never quite been rejected that forcefully, or publicly, before.

It would be a cold day in the desert before he would have anything to do with her again.

He brought his focus back to the present and Aunt April. "I wanted to talk to you. But I couldn't ask you to stop working, and I could hardly stay and do nothing while you did all the work."

"Your mother raised you right, son," Aunt April said with a smile.

She and Uncle Edgar had celebrated their fiftieth wedding anniversary five years prior, which had been the last time Smith had seen her.

They had come to the Cities to do it, and he had made the time to go to the party the family had organized. When he'd been in the Air Force, he'd missed enough family gatherings for the rest of his life.

Aunt April and Uncle Edgar had the kind of marriage that everyone aspired to. One where they laughed together, still held hands, and smiled into each other's eyes, sharing jokes and whispering in each other's ears like they were teens.

That's the way they'd always acted, and Smith loved seeing them.

Unfortunately, they were the only couple he knew who was like that.

Most couples could barely stand each other by the time they'd been married for more than a few years. Maybe he just lived in a high-risk bubble because way more than half of his married friends had been divorced at least once.

"We could have talked while we were working. You should have said something." Aunt April put the lid on the garbage can and brushed her hands together.

"I didn't want to do it in front of an audience. It's about the farm."

Understanding dawned in her eyes. "Let me text your Uncle Edgar and tell him that if he hasn't already started for me, I need a few more minutes."

Uncle Edgar had taken some kids home and returned some borrowed roasting pans, which had contained meatballs and chicken corn soup for the wedding. Aunt April would never dream of sending them home with people dirty, so she made sure they'd gotten washed and dried and were in better shape going home than they had been when they had been brought. That was just Aunt April's way.

She glanced at her phone when it buzzed. "We're good. He got stuck talking to Sonny Hastings and will be there for a bit anyway."

Aunt April chuckled like the idea of Uncle Edgar getting waylaid by a man who wanted to talk to him was funny.

Smith supposed it probably was to her, since Uncle Edgar would definitely be known as the strong, silent type. But he got on well with Aunt April, who was his exact opposite in that area at least.

Now that he thought about it, he and Uncle Edgar had a lot in common. Although, ten years ago he would have said he was more like Aunt April.

Life had a way of shaping a person.

"I told you that if you came out, the farm would be yours. You're family. And you're the only one who's interested in it."

"I'm the only one who's desperate enough to want to live in North Dakota."

"That might be true," Aunt April said with a laugh. "But she grows on you. In fact, I think you'll find you love it here. There's definitely a wildness about the place that really makes you fall in love."

She was talking about North Dakota like it was a woman. Maybe some people thought about the land that way, but he'd grown up in the city, and he didn't. He thought about it as a means to an end. Right now, he needed a place to live, needed a job or a way to make a living, the farm was free, and that was all he needed to know. That, and it was far away from Kylie.

"Maybe so. But you also said there were some stipulations."

"Yes. Before I ever talked to you, there was someone who had approached me about living on the farm. It wasn't good for the farmhouse to be empty, and your Uncle Edgar and I had just moved to town. I told them they could stay in it as long as they fixed anything that was broken and paid the electric and taxes. They've held up their end of the bargain for almost two years. I can't just kick them out."

This was a circumstance he had not seen coming.

But Smith wasn't going to allow the idea of sharing the house with some kind of housemate, someone crazy enough to live alone in North Dakota, to scare him off.

"Is this person safe? They're not a serial killer or anything?" He was being a little bit sarcastic, but he supposed it was a question that he needed to know. He knew how to use firearms, of course, but he didn't want to have to sleep with one under his pillow and with one eye open because of his houseguest/roommate.

"Of course. I wouldn't have allowed them to move in if not. They grew up in the area, moved to Rockerton for a bit, lost their job, and want to scale back and live their dream."

"All right then. Good for him."

"Actually, it's a she." His aunt bit her lip. "And that was the other thing I wanted to talk to you about."

"Yeah?"

"I really can't let the two of you live out there together. I mean, I know it's something that people do all the time nowadays—"

"No. I get it. Small towns." He said it almost sarcastically, but after what had gone down with Kylie, he had kind of gone back to his roots. After all, if he didn't want to be around people who acted like she did, there needed to be some kind of foundation from which he operated. It couldn't be that everyone did what was right in their own eyes. Otherwise, it would end up being chaos since Kylie didn't see anything wrong with what she had done. If there was no moral standard, there was nothing that was off-limits. It was just a matter of whatever some human thought shouldn't be done, and everyone would be forced to follow arbitrary laws that would shift depending on who was in power.

He hadn't thought of all that overnight; it had taken him a bit. Of course, when a person hit bottom, that was always when they turned to God, wasn't it?

He supposed he was no different than millions of men through the ages. Men who hadn't felt like they needed the Lord until they completely failed on their own. Regardless, he wasn't going to fight his aunt on that.

"I don't want to live with a woman I'm not married to. I get it. I'll give her plenty of time to move out, and I can find a place to stay until she does."

Jonah and Gideon would be fine if he stayed with them. Their house was big enough for more. Baker and Zeke would be coming eventually, possibly Eli if they could talk him into it, but for now, they would have a bedroom for him.

Aunt April shifted uncomfortably. "I... I can't ask her to move out."

"You can't?" Her words made the thoughts in his brain stop short. He was ready to spend a little bit of time away from the farm, in order to be able to move onto it, but...if the woman wasn't moving out...

"I never told her she would have to. I didn't realize you were going to be interested in the farm when I told her she could stay. It wouldn't be right of me to just spring on her that she has to go."

"No. Of course not. We'll give her plenty of time. Three months? Six months?"

His aunt shook her head, and Smith's heart sank. Aunt April was the sweetest lady in the entire world, but when she got stubborn about something, there was no changing her mind.

"No. You're welcome to move out there, and she is welcome to stay, but only if you two get married."

Smith had never quite had a moment like that before in his life. A moment where he could actually feel his jaw opening to the point where it bounced on the ground while his eyeballs bulged and his eyebrows hit his hairline.

Then, he got a hold of himself. He had to have misheard.

"I'm sorry. I thought you said I had to marry her." He laughed. But his laugh sounded hollow and kind of died away as Aunt April's expression remained serious.

"That's exactly what I said."

"What? Is she some kind of...odd woman?" He couldn't say ugly. He didn't really mean that. He knew that a woman's looks had nothing to do with her heart. Look at Kylie. She was gorgeous. But her heart was as black as sin. "She can't find someone who will take her?"

"I think everyone around here is odd," Aunt April stated, very unhelpfully. It didn't ease Smith's mind at all.

"Well, I can't argue with that."

"You aren't exactly normal yourself."

He couldn't argue with that, either. She was right. There wasn't anything "normal" about him.

"Are you saying she would ask the same question about me? What's wrong with me that no one else will have me?"

His aunt raised a brow, and Smith pulled his lip back, crossed his arms over his chest, and looked away.

Sometimes he wondered that himself. What was wrong with him? Why did women seem to like him okay at first and then either ghost him or decide that he looked like the perfect person to take advantage of?

He hadn't found anyone who was willing to stick with him. Well, no one of marriageable age. Aunt April had always been a rock in his life, even if he hadn't always talked to her.

"All right. I see your point. Does she know about me?"

"No. I've been busy organizing this wedding, and I haven't had time to say anything to her. You didn't exactly give me a lot of notice."

"I'm sorry." He sighed and ran a hand through his hair, hooking it on the back of his neck, looking off in the distance. The community center was not on the edge of town, but since there was only one main street through Sweet Water, standing at the back of it he could look out over open fields, as far as the eye could see. Only it was dark, and in the darkness, he just saw what felt like a million stars, brighter than anything he'd ever seen in the city. Not that he even noticed the stars in the city, but the night was black, the stars bright, and somehow the sky felt bigger than it ever had anywhere else he'd been. Even in Montana, the lights from the base typically kept him from being able to see the sky, although when he had been stationed in Montana, he hadn't exactly spent his time stargazing.

"I wasn't giving you a hard time. But I really would have told her if you had given me more time, or if I hadn't been involved in the wedding. If you like, I can talk to her tomorrow. You said you were coming, but I didn't know what day this week to expect you."

"I know. Everything was kind of up in the air." Basically, he made the decision to go, and he planned to leave as soon as he had everything taken care of, whenever that turned out to be. Hopefully before his money ran out.

He made that deadline, just barely.

Be that as it may, he hadn't expected to step into something like this when he got to North Dakota.

"I really don't want to get married again." To say the least. The very, very least. He'd been married before, once. To Kylie. She had been his business partner, too. He'd thought they'd been a true love match and were soulmates, but she'd only been using him.

His marriage to Kylie had been just as much of a disaster as every other relationship in his life.

They'd barely been married for three years before she decided she made a huge mistake and left him, taking everything she could in the process, which turned out to be a lot.

Last he'd heard, she'd been married again and divorced, with that marriage lasting less than an arctic summer, and had moved on to someone new before the ink on the divorce papers was dry. But he didn't keep tabs on her and really had no idea what she was up to now. He just viewed her as one more example in a long line of proof that he was not relationship material.

"I'm not trying to force you into it. But I think you understand that I can't go back on my word. I told her she could stay there, and I didn't give her an end date. I told her as long as she kept things up and paid the electric and the taxes, she was good."

"Then she might not even agree to marry me." Somehow that statement felt less like relief than what he thought it should.

"No," Aunt April said, slowly like she was still thinking. "But I can tell her the place rightfully belongs to my nephew, and that if she wants to stay there, she can't live with you and not be married to you."

That didn't exactly make sense to Smith. He wasn't sure he understood the intricate details that differentiated between telling her she couldn't stay and telling her she couldn't stay unless she got married to him. How one would be okay and one not. If he had to choose, the option where she had to get married would be the one that was not socially acceptable.

Maybe that was part of the reason he had such issues with relationships. He had a hard time figuring out what was socially acceptable, especially to women. And recognizing the details that made something off, at least to them.

"All right." He wasn't sure what he was saying all right about. Was he agreeing to get married? He didn't think so. Maybe he was just agreeing that Aunt April would say something to the woman who was living in his house.

He couldn't deny the hope blossoming in his chest. Sweet and strong. Possibly the woman wouldn't want to marry him. In fact, maybe he could make sure she wouldn't want to marry him.

"Is it okay if I go out to the place now? I mean, I can sleep in the barn or something."

"I think it's okay to stay in a spare bedroom. It's just not appropriate for you two to live together. I know we're kind of splitting hairs, but it's one thing for you to stay at a place because you need to for a short amount of time, it's another thing for you to move in."

"All right. I can roll with that. I'll go out tonight and say something to her—"

"No. Please don't. You can go out tonight, but I want to be the one to talk to her. So both of you can come see me in the morning. I have two ladies that I'm working with on their marriages, and we always meet at the community center in the back room at nine o'clock on Saturdays. We'll be there until lunch. You can see us any time."

"All right. I'll let her know, and I won't say anything about marriage." He wouldn't need to. He'd just be himself, which apparently was enough to drive women away from him, and he shouldn't have any trouble getting this one to wish she would have moved out two weeks ago and never even met him.

Chapter 5

A brielle sat on her front porch, a cup of chamomile tea in her hand, a candle flickering in the kitchen window.

It had been quite a day. A long one.

She didn't have any animals, although she'd been kicking around the idea of getting a dog. She'd have to talk to Miss April about that. So she hadn't. She didn't want to push her luck. After all, Miss April had been extremely gracious in allowing her to stay on the ranch for basically free.

Of course, she watched multiple do-it-yourself videos online and fixed things all winter long.

She didn't own a TV, and it was crazy the amount of things a person could get done when they didn't waste time giving their brain candy instead of using it on constructive projects.

At least that was her opinion anyway. Her official opinion. The reality was she just couldn't afford a TV.

She tucked one foot under her and used her toe to gently push the swing back and forth as she took another sip of her tea. She'd worked in her garden before the wedding and had everything packed up and ready to go to the farmers market in the morning.

And she had been able to catch Billy before the wedding celebration ended. The pig had been nowhere in sight, but Billy had come quite willingly and had loved all the attention he'd gotten from the children.

The crazy steer seemed to know just when to get away though, and after she helped clean everything up, she realized he was no longer in the petting area. She couldn't find him anywhere.

She supposed she should be used to it by now. He always seemed to manage to escape, and she figured he never would really belong to anyone.

That was probably why no one in the town actually knew where he came from or who he truly belonged to.

Or maybe the person who owned him just didn't want to admit it because they couldn't keep him in.

Regardless, she felt satisfied in her soul, the way she always did after a good day of hard work, where she was tired and weary but peaceful and feeling like she had contributed in a positive way to the world that day.

She pulled the blanket a little tighter around her. In the evenings, she tried to use as little electricity as possible unless she was working on a project. It kept the bill down, and she loved candlelight anyway.

She'd no sooner thought that when a flash of light brought her eyes up, straining to look down the driveway.

Was that lightning? It was spring, and it wasn't uncommon to get storms, even severe ones. But she hadn't heard anything about severe weather today, which did not mean that it wouldn't happen.

But no, they were headlights. She could see them clearly now coming up the lane.

Who in the world would be visiting her at this time of the evening?

Living here alone, a woman by herself, out away from anyone else, did pose its risks, and she wished now she would have spoken to Miss April about that dog.

This was only the fourth time people had come to visit her after dark. Each time, it had been fine. Twice, it had been Miss April coming to check on her, and once, it had been Teagan and her best friend, Deuce.

It seemed like Teagan and Deuce were always together, although they weren't a couple. Just great friends.

Sometimes Abrielle wished she had a good friend like Deuce.

It seemed like everyone but Teagan and Deuce could see that they were meant to be together.

Abrielle had never confronted Teagan about it, but once when they'd been talking about something else, Teagan had confided to Abrielle that Deuce had a crazy crush on a girl from high school and had never quite given up hope of someday having her choose him.

Abrielle had gotten the idea that Teagan wouldn't mind if Deuce set his sights on her, but she had figured it to be impossible.

There was nothing more sad than unrequited love, so Abrielle hadn't probed deeper to find out if her suspicions were true. Teagan and Deuce always looked happy together, and Teagan never seemed melancholy, so maybe it was just the musings of a romantic.

The vehicle got closer, until it stopped right next to the porch and shut off. The lights went out, and Abrielle's hand tightened on her mug of tea. It wasn't Teagan because it was an unfamiliar pickup.

Abrielle wasn't afraid, just wary. She was alone in what basically amounted to the middle of nowhere. She wasn't afraid at night by herself, but she also knew that the most serious threats to her were of the two-legged variety.

Most likely any serious threats wouldn't drive up and park right in front of her porch, but a person never knew. That didn't keep Abrielle's heart from crashing into her ribs with every rapid beat.

The door opened, a male figure got out, and it slammed behind him as he walked up to the porch.

The moon was half and must have just come out from behind a cloud, shining directly onto the porch, and they saw each other clearly at that moment.

"You!" the man said.

She blinked. "You?"

It was the man who had yelled at her on the sidewalk. Who had insulted her with every breath he took at the wedding. The one she had embarrassed, not necessarily deliberately, but she had to get away.

She didn't expect him to understand. In her experience, men didn't understand or care.

And in particular, this man wouldn't. It seemed like everything she said he took as offensive.

"I should have figured." The man huffed out a breath, turned as though he were going to walk away, then turned halfway back, shoving his hands in his pockets and leaning his head back, as though the answer to some difficult question was written on the ceiling of her porch.

"I take it you didn't realize you were coming out here to see me? Are you lost?"

He didn't say anything more, and she didn't know what else to ask.

Finally, he spoke. "I'm staying the night. Tell me which bedroom is yours and I'll choose a different one."

"Wait. What? You're just coming in here and announcing that you're staying at my house?"

"Yeah. That's what I just did. If you don't tell me what bedroom I can take, I will choose my own."

"You can't just come in here and decide that you're going to stay. This is my house."

"No. April and Edgar Rafton own this house."

"But I'm renting it."

"You're not paying anything for it."

She stopped with her mouth open. He must have spoken with Miss April. How else would he know she wasn't paying anything for it? Miss April was the only one who knew. And Mr. Edgar. "You're going to have to explain what's going on."

"I don't have to explain anything." He walked back down off the porch, going to the passenger side of his truck and pulling a duffel bag out of it.

She'd gone from shock to anger just that fast. No. Anger was not nearly a strong enough word to describe how she was feeling. Furious. Aghast, like she wanted to grab his head and rip it off his shoulders.

Okay. Maybe she didn't exactly want to do bodily harm to him, but it was close. How dare he just come in here and announce he was staying at her house without giving an explanation the way a normal, decent person would?

"I'm not going to allow you to just walk into my house."

"You have no right to stop me." He didn't even look at her as he put his hand on the doorknob and pulled it open.

She jumped off the swing without even realizing it, her blanket dropping to the floor, her tea spilling, but she didn't notice that, either.

He ignored her, and the door slammed shut behind him.

So angry she could barely see, she set her cup down on the banister and pulled out her phone, her thumbs striking the protective glass with audible jabs.

> **Did you give someone permission to stay here tonight?**

She hit send, hating to bother Miss April at this time of the evening but not knowing what else to do.

> **My nephew was going to stay there tonight, and then you and he are going to come in and talk to me in the morning at the community center in the back room. Didn't he tell you that?**

It was true. Miss April had given that man permission. And he was her nephew.

Her *nephew*.

Abrielle took a deep breath. That could mean anything. Not just that Miss April was giving him the farm and kicking her off.

She tried to regulate her anger, which was now mixed with a heavy dose of fear, and send back a reasonable response.

> No. He must have forgotten.

She didn't know why she was covering for him. Or defending him. Or...

She didn't know what she was doing. She just couldn't rant about him over a text to his aunt. Even if he was a jerk, a really big jerk, she just couldn't make herself tell Miss April. Surely the facts would come out tomorrow without her having to explain it, if he was actually planning on meeting with his aunt.

Whether he was or not, she would. He was right that she didn't have the right to kick him out of the house that wasn't exactly hers, but she was paying for the electricity and the taxes. And Miss April hadn't said anything to her about an end date. Just that she could live there as long as she paid—and she had paid. Several months, she'd eaten nothing but boxed mac and cheese and dried beans in order to have the money to pay the taxes and electricity.

She should have some say in who got to sleep in her house.

Maybe he was supposed to ask permission and hadn't. Or maybe he was supposed to discuss it with her and just chose not to.

She had trained herself when she was working in the corporate world to think the best of everyone. It hadn't always been easy, and she hadn't always been successful, but she'd avoided a lot of the office drama by determining that she wasn't going to think badly of anyone.

Sometimes there was a reasonable explanation. Sometimes people were hurting, or going through a hard time, or having some kind of problem that wasn't apparent on the surface.

So many times, she'd been grateful that she had been kind when something had come out. She watched as other people had struggled with their guilt for being unkind and finding out later that the person had been going through a divorce, or their mother had cancer, or they had lost a child.

She couldn't imagine what in the world this man—she'd never even learned his name—was going through. He seemed strong enough to withstand anything, but sometimes the people who put on a brave front were the most vulnerable inside.

Still, her anger wasn't quite under control, although she bent down, picking up her blanket and folding it, putting it over her arm before she grabbed her teacup and walked inside.

He had turned on the light, and she could see where he tracked his muddy boots through the kitchen and hall and she assumed the stairs as the light shone on the chips of mud which clearly showed where he'd walked.

The anger she had been trying to tamp down boiled back up.

She dropped her cup in the sink with a clank. It didn't break, but she wasn't sure she would have cared if it had. It would have been satisfying, almost.

The man was arrogant beyond words. And inconsiderate. An insufferable jerk.

She couldn't believe he was related to the sweet and kind Miss April.

Knowing she wasn't going to be sleepy for a very long time, she grabbed the book she had been reading from the coffee table in the living room, intending to take it upstairs and not show up again until it was time to head to town in the morning.

She'd skip breakfast. It would be better to be hungry than to actually have to face that terrible person again. The one who made her blood boil just by breathing.

The trail of mud went the entire way up the stairs, the lights in the hall had been left on, and she could see they went straight to her room.

Of course.

Well, that wasn't going to happen. He could tell that she was already sleeping there. Her clothes were on the chair beside the bed and her things were on the dresser for starters. Surely it wouldn't be too much to ask for him to find a different room. There was one other bed, although it was single and wasn't made. It would work for him for tonight, though.

If he'd been kind or at least deferential, she would have helped him find sheets.

Her anger made her breath come fast and her hands sweat. They shook a little as she grabbed the knob and jerked the door open, taking three stomping, determined steps before she came up short.

Somehow the man had managed to drop his duffel, remove his shirt and his pants, and stood there in his—

She lifted her eyes. Whatever he was standing in. Or not in.

Now she wanted to cry. She didn't want a mostly naked man in her bedroom. She wanted him out. Out of her bedroom, out of her house, and most of all, out of her life. She never wanted to see him again.

"This is my room. You can find one of the other bedrooms for yourself. There are four other ones." Her anger made her words come out in a rambling kind of way, making her feel stupid and even angrier that she couldn't even manage to sound like an intelligent human being because of this man.

It is your choice to allow him to upset you.

No! Any normal person would be upset at behavior like this.

Are you going to allow him to control you?

He's not controlling. I'm just reacting the way any sane person would!

She shouldn't be having an argument with herself. Even if she knew the better part of herself was right.

With her eyes glued on the ceiling, she took three calming breaths, because she knew her brain was correct.

She could choose to not be upset by this man. She could choose to be calm and peaceful no matter what he did. If she got upset, she was just allowing his actions to control her and cause her stress and strain.

"Are you going to leave?" There. Her voice sounded almost rational.

"No. I'm not going to walk around the house in my underwear."

She couldn't help it. She coughed up a laugh. What did it matter if he walked around the house? She was the only one who was around to see him. And if he walked around the house in his underwear, she wouldn't be seeing him because she would be staying in her room!

She took another deep breath. Her thoughts had gotten a little wild and crazy on that last idea. Because he was being so, so, *so* unreasonable.

"You think this is funny?" He sounded dumbfounded.

Hooray. Her brain was right. She could get angry, or she could flip the tables on him.

She liked the idea of flipping the tables on him. So she went ahead with what she had started and giggled.

"Yeah. If you walk around the house in your underwear, nobody's going to see you." She said that while looking straight into his eyes, emphasizing it like it was the simplest concept in the world. "Because I'm here. And I'm the only other person in the house."

"Maybe you'll want to leave then. That way I won't be awkwardly standing here in my underwear thinking that you're enjoying the view."

"There's not much to look at." She didn't mean to sound like a snob, and she kept a smile on her face. Maybe she should have kept her mouth shut, because it sounded a little mean. She didn't mean to be mean. Truly. She was better than that.

"What are we, junior high?"

"I thought we were slightly younger, because I think you're about three when you learn that when you walk into the house and you have mud on your boots, you take them off and leave them at the door."

She tilted her head, crossed her arms over her chest, and lifted her brows at him. She was right, and he knew it. He had the grace to look slightly ashamed.

"I wanted to take a shower before I go to bed. Are you gonna watch or are you gonna leave?"

"Are you really staying in this room? You do realize this is my bed? I slept there last night. Actually I've been sleeping there for two years. You really want to sleep in my bed, on the same sheets I've been sleeping on? Isn't that a little...weird?"

"This is not the first time today I've been accused of being weird. I think I'm gonna embrace it."

"All right. Go hug yourself. If you don't mind, I'll grab some clothes and get my stuff out of the bathroom, since...this is my room."

"Actually. I do mind. I'm getting cold standing here, and I'm going to get in the shower before I freeze to death. I'm also tired. I want to go to bed."

"But it's my stuff that's in the bathroom." She tried not to sound like she was gritting her teeth while she was talking, but she was definitely gritting her teeth while she was talking.

Don't let him control you. You don't have to get angry. You can be happy. Choose joy.

Was that possible? Was it humanly possible for someone to not want to murder someone who had done what this man had done to her today?

Had she actually thought he was good-looking? She was so wrong.

Okay. That could almost be humor, because even though she was extremely angry at him, more angry than she could ever remember being at anyone in her life before, he actually wasn't bad looking. Too bad his personality didn't match his looks. It was a good thing that she did not predicate her affections upon someone who merely looked good but didn't have character and integrity.

She thought that last bit as she stood alone in the room, the bathroom door closing in her face as he disappeared inside.

Chapter 6

"My nephew is coming later today along with Abrielle."

Miss April settled herself in her chair as Helen stopped and looked at her.

They always met at 9 o'clock on Saturday mornings for their quilting and marriage counseling sessions.

Helen looked forward to them. She had been struggling in her marriage to Aiden, her high school sweetheart.

He had changed since high school, changed a lot. They'd raised children together, and she felt like she had done everything she could to be the best wife and mother she could be, while he had slowly changed into someone she didn't even recognize and honestly didn't like. She tried to love him anyway, biblical love, but she really looked forward to her Saturday sessions with Miss April, who had been married for more than fifty years and had so much wisdom and knowledge and advice that Helen just ate it up.

June, the other lady who came to their Saturday morning sessions, was in a similar situation. She and her husband were struggling, and Helen often wondered if June was considering the same solution she was. Divorce.

Miss April hadn't been trying to talk them out of it, she just discussed with them what the Bible said and how they were supposed to act as Christians all the time, which included how they acted toward their spouses and how they treated them.

June lay cut flowers out on the table in front of her. She was going to be decorating several wreaths for her front door, and if Helen knew June, she would be giving one to Miss April and to Helen.

As for herself, Helen was making several decorations for the annual Sweet Water summer festival. She always had a booth and usually made enough money to buy all of her Christmas gifts that year.

"I didn't know your nephew was in town," June said casually, echoing Helen's thoughts.

"He just got in last night. You might have seen them at the wedding. He was the one with the garter."

"Oh, poor boy!" Helen said without thinking. She felt so bad for him being embarrassed in front of everyone when Abrielle had hurried off. There had been some intense conversation between the two of them, so Helen couldn't exactly fault Abrielle for what she had done. She didn't know what they were saying.

She knew from experience that sometimes men could be quite mean and could seem unaffected by the things they were saying, while the woman they were talking to went off in tears.

"I don't know what happened there, and while I did talk to Abrielle later, I didn't talk to her about that. I don't think she knew he was my nephew, and we had some other things to discuss."

"I see. So they're meeting here today, and Abrielle still doesn't know that he's your nephew?"

"He stayed out at the farmhouse last night."

"With Abrielle?" June asked.

"Yes. I told him it was okay for one night. I also had told him that the farmhouse was basically his, since no one else in the family wanted it. But Abrielle has been living there for two years. I can't just kick her out."

"I'm so glad you won't. That would be unfair." Helen spoke with feeling. So often decisions were made by people thinking about what was best for themselves. They didn't actually think about what was right or what would be best for other people.

She found herself doing that sometimes. She wanted to live a life that put others first, but it was hard, because it seemed like society in general encouraged people to make decisions that worked for themselves and not care about how they affected others.

She loved that Miss April once again lived up to what Helen thought of her. That she was a godly woman who tried to live what the Bible said and not what the world told her to do.

"What are you going to do?" June asked, picking up a flower and looking at it carefully before setting it down with a group of other flowers.

"I'm going to tell them that they have to get married if they want the ranch."

Helen dropped her glue gun onto the floor. She bent down to pick it up, bumping her head on the table.

The pain thumped through her as she held onto the glue gun, closing her eyes, waiting for it to subside.

She took a breath, straightening up slowly with the gun held carefully in her hand. She set it down on the table, deliberately, before she said, "I thought you said you were going to tell them they had to get married."

"That's what I said."

"But... Do they even know each other?"

"As far as I know, they met yesterday at the wedding. I could be wrong."

"You're wrong. We met about an hour before the wedding on the sidewalk when her cow just about gored me. I was this close to having my intestines lying on the ground and bleeding out in front of Patty's Diner."

Helen looked toward the door and watched as Smith, Miss April's nephew, walked in.

She had seen him yesterday at the wedding, but he was even taller than she remembered and rather handsome too. He wasn't smiling, and again Helen wondered if maybe he had said something to Abrielle that had caused her to run, even though it had looked like Abrielle had deliberately embarrassed him.

"I see. So she was chasing Billy?" Miss April said casually.

"Yeah."

"Do you think you might be a little dramatic?" Miss April looked over her glasses at her nephew.

He shifted from one foot to the other. "I had a hole in my T-shirt from his horn."

"A big one?" Miss April asked easily.

"Well, no. But it was still a hole. The next thing that was lying next to that T-shirt was my skin."

"Did the horn touch your skin?"

"If I had been standing an inch closer, it would have."

"Or it might have veered even further away from you?"

Smith didn't say anything for just a second, and then he nodded. "We can theorize about it all we want to, but it almost ran me down, and I turned around just in time to see that woman chugging after it. She also almost ran me down."

"She's about half the size of you. I'm pretty sure she wouldn't have been running anything down." This was said by June, very casually. Without any heat, her words just sounded like fact.

"She might be little, but she's powerful."

He moved away from the door, maybe by instinct, since it opened two seconds later and Abrielle stepped through.

"Good morning, ladies. It's a beautiful day today. I think it's almost warm enough you guys can do this outside."

"I'd have to dig up an extension cord for my glue gun, which requires a little bit more energy than I want to exert right now." Helen had to return Abrielle's smile. She looked as bright and happy as Smith looked glum.

She closed her mouth, pressing her lips tight together. She didn't want to accidentally spill any beans about a marriage if these two didn't know about it. And from the antagonistic way they seemed to be deliberately ignoring each other, she would guess they didn't.

"Come on in and sit down. Sometimes I talk better when my hands are busy, so if you don't mind, I'm going to continue crocheting this dog sweater while we chat." Miss April smiled, not really asking permission but nodding to two chairs on the other side of the table.

The chairs she nodded at were side by side. Smith walked around, grabbed one of the chairs, and moved it to the far end of the table before he sat down.

Abrielle walked around the other side of the table, grabbed the chair that was left, carried it to the opposite end of the table, and sat down.

Helen hid a smile, tucking her head down and pretending to study the flower she held in her hand, although she couldn't have told anyone if it was purple or yellow or black.

This was going to be an interesting morning.

Chapter 7

"Did you sleep well?" Miss April asked, and Helen didn't lift her head to see who she was talking to.

"I slept great. I had no idea that the single bed in the spare bedroom was so comfortable. I think I'm going to stay there from now on. I just fell in love. And that room. The sun came in first thing this morning. It woke me up, and it was glorious. I watched the sunrise from my bed. It's a beautiful room. I don't know why I was staying in that other one."

"Because it has a bathroom. There wasn't a single inch of area on the sink where I could actually set anything down with all the tubes and potions and poisons you had sitting on it. I hope you don't mind, but I put your stuff in the garbage can along with the three rather ratty-looking bras that were hanging over the shower. They looked like something my grandmother might have bought at a yard sale to use as dust rags. If you want them, you can fish them out later, although I might have spit in the trash can. I can't remember."

"I love the bathroom downstairs better anyway. Maybe I'll just start using that one instead," Abrielle said, her smile never dimming.

Helen's eyes grew big. Taking all of her stuff off the sink and putting it in the garbage can was something her husband Aiden would do.

Smith just didn't seem like the kind of man who would normally do something like that, but it sounded like there were also deeper issues between these two that might have caused him to be deliberately provoking her.

Helen wasn't any expert on relationships, although maybe she was an expert on surviving them, but she would say that Abrielle had decided to be happy no matter what, and Smith had decided to do whatever it took to make her angry.

The plot thickened.

Helen decided to forget about pretending to look at her flowers. The wreaths could wait, and she set them on the table, folding her hands in her lap and staring at the couple in front of them.

She noticed that June had also dropped her hands to her lap and was not pretending to be busy any longer.

"You put her things in the garbage can?"

"Maybe," Smith mumbled.

"I'm sorry." Miss April looked over at Abrielle. "Smith is many things, but he's never been mean. Still, I think I understand what the problem is."

She lifted a brow at her nephew, who, if Helen was a judge, was getting a little hot under the collar.

"I would love it if you'd explain it to me, because he's acting like I personally offended him. And all I did was chase my steer, which, possibly, *allegedly*, put a small hole in his T-shirt. He's been angry at me ever since."

"Your cow almost killed me. It's enough to send any man over the edge."

"Okay, you two. This is the deal." Miss April's tone brokered no argument. "Smith is here in Sweet Water because the ranch that you are living on is our family ranch, and I told him that it would be his—" Abrielle opened her mouth, her eyes wide, but Miss Helen put her hand out. "—with some stipulations."

Abrielle closed her mouth but did not relax.

"What I didn't tell him before he came out here was that you were living here. He didn't know that until yesterday. And I told him the stipulations would be that you two would not live on that ranch as an unmarried couple. I know people do it all the time, and that's fine for them, but it's not something that we're even going to discuss. I'm not going to allow it, and that's final. So, last night I told Smith that the answer could be that the two of you would get married. I'm guessing," her eyes narrowed, and she looked at her nephew, "that he decided that he would be as mean as he could be to you so that whatever I told you this morning, you would say that you couldn't stand to be married to such a jerk, you would walk out, and he would have the ranch to himself."

Smith, a grown man, shuffled and squirmed in his chair like a third grader about to be punished for pulling his seatmate's hair.

"Smith?"

"Maybe. Something like that. I guess." He looked away, sighed, then looked back. His head turned toward Abrielle. "That's what I was doing. I was pretty mean. I'm sorry... I don't even know your name. It wasn't anything against you, it's just... I needed the ranch, and I've never had anything but bad experiences with women. So there's no way I'm getting married."

"There's no way I'm getting married either. Because the idea of being shackled to someone who would walk through the house with his boots on for the rest of my life is not something that I even want to begin to entertain."

Helen thought that might be the end of it, but Miss April put both hands up, one pointed toward Smith and one toward Abrielle.

"Okay, you two. I have a couple of things to say."

She waited, as though expecting them to protest, but Abrielle leaned back in her chair, her arms crossed over her chest. While her expression wasn't exactly mulish, she didn't look happy.

Smith shoved his hands in his jean pockets and rested his ankle on top of one knee.

"I'm listening," Smith said, his voice even, sounding unruffled, even though his expression said he was annoyed.

In Helen's opinion, he had less reason to be annoyed than Abrielle did. After all, he was the one who had been deliberately provoking her. Although she had embarrassed him at the wedding. And there was also the issue with the cow.

But Abrielle didn't look angry either, just stubbornly determined to do what she wanted and not be persuaded to go in any direction she wasn't okay with.

Helen could relate a little. She had been known to be stubborn herself. But she usually saw her stubbornness in a good way, because that was the reason she was still married. She was just too stubbornly determined to stay married and hadn't given up on her marriage when pretty much everyone around her would have told her that she should. In order to keep from getting that kind of advice from people, she refrained from talking about her marriage at all to anyone but June and Miss April.

"I'm listening, but you're not going to convince me of anything." Abrielle's lips pulled back in a bit of a forced-looking smile. The smile did very little to soften her words, if that was what the purpose was.

"I just want both of you to know that I wouldn't have suggested a marriage of convenience if I hadn't been completely sure of both of your character and integrity. However, I'm not the one getting married. So you each have to be sure of each other's character and integrity. As I'm sitting here, I think that since neither of you know each other, it might be wise to have a one-week trial period."

Miss April's lips pressed together like she wasn't sure of what she was going to say next, but then she took a deep breath.

"I do not want to have two unmarried people living together in my house. I know that's the way the world does things." She lifted a hand as though to head off any protest. Although, as Helen looked around, none of them were about to protest. She figured they probably all agreed, although she knew that people had a tendency to override their values and morals when they wanted something bad enough. "But it's not the way it's going to happen in a house that I own. Not judging. I'm just saying."

Helen's eyes swept the room again. No one had moved.

"But because, like I said, you two don't know each other, I think a week might be a good idea." She lifted her brows at Smith. "You can stay on the farm for a week. The two of you can discuss some things and see if this marriage might be a solution that will work for both of you. Something you can live with. Because when I suggest a marriage of convenience, I'm not talking about a temporary thing. It would be a covenant before God, one that should not be broken. So you need to think about that."

Smith moved his head almost imperceptibly, an acknowledgment of her words. Helen figured that to mean that he agreed with her about marriage being a covenant.

If she remembered correctly, Miss April had mentioned that Smith had been married once before, and his wife had walked out on him. Helen wasn't sure why. Whether it was Smith's fault for neglecting her or not taking care of her or even cheating on her, but she doubted that last one, or else Miss April wouldn't have suggested he get married to someone else. No matter whether he was her nephew or not.

The room was quiet, the silence not even broken by the ticking of any clock.

Finally, Abrielle spoke. "What was the other thing?"

Miss April lifted her brows and nodded, as though she were expecting that question eventually. "The other thing is that I have an offer on the farm. I haven't done anything with it, because I certainly didn't plan to sell it out from underneath you." She nodded her head at Abrielle who had gasped at the idea that the farm could be sold.

Her arms came down, and she leaned forward in her chair. "But—"

Miss April lifted her hand again in a stop signal. "Like I said, I hadn't been entertaining the idea at all. I knew Smith was coming, and as a family member, he really does have a right to the farm, just as much as you do for living on it for the last two years."

She lifted her brows, waiting for Abrielle to acknowledge with a twist of her lips that Miss April might have a point.

"As I was thinking about it, marriage seemed to be the best solution. Trust me, I didn't just come up with this on the spur of the moment. I have zero desire to ruin anyone's life. But both of you have good heads on your shoulders, both of you have character and integrity, and both of you are normally kind and willing to compromise." She gave Smith a sour look for the antics he'd engaged in for the last twelve hours.

He had the grace to look sheepish again.

"So, if it works for both of you, I'll give you a week. You can be out there on the farm together, and you'll have to compromise." She sighed. "I am not going to step into whose bedroom is whose, and who wears their shoes where, and who does what. Those are things you guys are going to have to work out. If, at the end of the week, you've decided that you cannot possibly get along, then both of you will leave the farm and I will accept the offer I was given two weeks ago." She looked first at Smith, who didn't look happy but seemed resigned, and then at Abrielle, who almost seemed angry. But there was also a certain amount of resignation in her posture. "Does that sound good to you two?"

Neither one of them said anything immediately. Helen figured that Miss April was one of the most patient people she knew, and she would wait as long as necessary.

To her surprise though, Miss April spoke again.

"And I don't think it would hurt for you two to listen today to both Helen and June. Maybe I'm putting them on the spot a little, but both of them could give you some wise advice about marriage, so it might not hurt for each of them to say a few words."

Smith lifted a shoulder. "I was planning on working on the farm today, getting settled in. But I wasn't planning on my life taking a direction quite like this." His voice held irony and possibly a bit of humor.

For the first time, Helen could see what Miss April had been talking about. He might actually be a good man.

"But if this is the direction it's going to go, I definitely won't turn down advice."

Miss April nodded, smiling, not a triumphant smile, but a smile that said she was happy that he was keeping an open mind about things.

When she turned to Abrielle, though, her face looked a little bit more stubborn, less open.

"I don't know. I'm not against advice, and I'll listen, but... I guess being nice to someone and not allowing them to get on your last nerve for twelve hours is one thing. But to be stuck with someone like that for the rest of your life is still something I am so not interested in."

"I said I was sorry. I'm not usually like that. But Aunt April was right. I thought if we were going to come in here today, you would outright refuse me, and then I would have the place to myself. I didn't realize she was going to make having the farm contingent on the both of us doing it together."

Abrielle seemed to listen to him, although she didn't look at him. Then she turned completely away, looking at the back wall, her face turned from everyone before she crossed her arms over her chest as though in protection and said, "I guess I can give it a week. But I'm not holding out a whole lot of hope that this is going to work."

Miss April took a deep breath, then she blew it out. "Helen? Do you have something to say about that?"

Helen felt her eyes widen, and she sat up a little taller in her chair, her fingers gripping the fake flower that she had picked up just to have something to hold. She wasn't used to people asking for her advice. It had always been her seeking advice for her marriage.

But then she thought of something that she wished that someone would have told her husband.

"I guess my advice would be for Smith."

Smith jerked his head at her, and although she was rather intimidated, she said what she thought.

"I wish someone would have explained to my husband that when he was unkind to me, it hurt. And being unkind for a year, or however long, couldn't just be erased by a few words and one day of being nice. He seems to think that he can treat me however he wants to and an apology and a nice dinner should be able to make up for anything." She took a breath. She wasn't used to saying those things to other people. And she didn't want to malign her husband. No matter whether he deserved it or not. "I guess I wish he could just be nice, and he could forget about the apologies and the dinners."

Smith nodded. And he looked guilty, like he knew he deserved that.

Miss April smiled. "Sometimes it's helpful to get advice from people who have been there." She lifted her brows and looked over at June. "Do you have anything to add?"

June's lips lifted up, and her eyes looked off in the distance for a moment before they settled on Abrielle. "I guess I could say something to you. It seems fair that if Smith gets a word, you should too."

Abrielle smiled. It was hard not to, since June was such a sweet person. Just knowing a little bit of what was going on with her husband, Helen's heart went out to her. Someone who was so kind didn't deserve to be treated the way her husband treated her.

But of course, June didn't mention anything about that.

"If you decide to go through with it, no matter what kind of marriage, a convenient marriage or whatever, it is. Marriage is marriage. And you want to train yourself to be more encouraging and less critical. To have more happiness and less complaints. Be more of a builder and less the kind of person who tears your husband down. A wife has a very special place in a man's life, and honestly, the kind of man he becomes can be greatly influenced by the kind of wife he has. I don't think women understand how big of an influence, how big of a difference they can make in the world. We...we want the glory for ourselves. And we don't see that sometimes the place where we're most needed is the place where no one is going to notice us."

Her eyes dropped, and she looked at her lap.

Every time Helen listened to June, she was inspired anew at how much June had taken what God's word said and applied it to her life. And how big of a blessing she had become to others because of that. Knowing a little of the background of June's marriage and life made her attitude and her actions that much more inspiring.

Her words must have had the same effect on Abrielle as they always had on Helen. The mulish look had slipped from her face, and her eyes were downcast even while she nodded slowly.

Helen didn't smile, although she was tempted to. So often people, herself included, wanted to live for themselves, and a gentle reminder, humble and low, just as June had delivered, was timely and welcome to make a person remember that if they were truly living what they believed, they wouldn't be living for themselves.

"Thank you, ladies. Both of you are absolutely right on. Do you two have any questions?" Miss April lifted her eyes to Abrielle and Smith.

Abrielle shook her head. "I'm willing to do one week." That was all she said. A simple statement, profound in its simplicity. She wasn't giving a lot of contingencies, and she wasn't blaming or pointing fingers at anyone anymore.

"Me too. And I will not be deliberately trying to make anyone angry at me." Smith's voice held contrition, and Helen thought that maybe Miss April knew what she was doing, and this whole convenient marriage thing might actually work.

"All right, you two. I'd like to see you next Saturday right here, and we'll see what you have to say."

"If that's it, I need to go." Abrielle stood, looking at Miss April as though waiting for permission to actually leave.

"I'm done. Thanks for coming."

"Thanks for allowing me to live at your place. And...thanks for coming up with a solution that's fair to both of us." Abrielle seemed to be very aware that it was well within Miss April's right to take the farm from her and give it to her nephew without any retribution for Abrielle at all.

"I'll be back here next week," Smith said as he stood.

"We'll see you then." Miss April stood with them while Helen and June also walked over to say goodbye.

Helen figured things might get pretty interesting out at the farm this week.

Chapter 8

The door slammed in his face, and Smith didn't bother to turn around to see what the ladies thought of that as he yanked it open and hurried out after the woman who'd just slammed it.

The irony of the whole situation hadn't been lost on him. He'd just spent the last twelve hours making everything harder on himself by being a jerk to the person he now needed to get along with in order to have a place to live.

It hadn't been something he had enjoyed, either.

Well, maybe the part where she had walked into the bedroom. He hadn't been expecting that. He figured they would have a conversation around the closed door.

She'd been cute when she'd been flustered, and he kinda thought it was something that, in a normal situation, they probably would have laughed about.

He had the impression that she was the kind of person who laughed about a lot of things.

Part of him, a big part of him, knew he had made a mistake. She had struck him as one of those crazy ladies at first, but the more time he'd spent around her, his brain had been telling him she was the kind of woman he'd been looking for.

Not that he wanted to get married. Nothing changed there for him, but his back was against the wall and he didn't have too many other options.

He'd been counting on the family ranch and had been putting all of his effort into coming to North Dakota and making a fresh start.

"Lady." He realized they'd never even been introduced. "Hey, lady. I don't even know your name," he finally said in frustration.

Her steps slowed, her back still toward him. "It's Abrielle. I'm sorry, but I'm already late for the farmers market."

"I can help you."

He hadn't meant to say that, but after the words were out, he realized that was probably the best thing he could have said. Because it brought her up short, and there was definitely interest in her eyes as she looked over her shoulder

"Really?"

He nodded, walking slowly toward her like she was an animal that could be scared away. His hand came out. "I'm Smith. I'm sorry I didn't introduce myself properly. But it really is nice to meet you."

That made her lips work out. "Really? You say that like you're trying to convince yourself of it."

"No. I'm trying to convince you."

She looked down at his hand, then back up into his eyes before her hand came out, and she clasped his.

Hers was much smaller than his, and it disappeared completely as their hands went up and down, hers with a nice firm grip before they slid apart again.

Odd that he felt strangely like he was losing something of value as her hand pulled away.

"Well, you haven't convinced me, but I'm definitely interested in your offer of help."

"I meant it." He took a breath. "I also meant that apology. I'm sorry for being a jerk. Aunt April was right. I... I knew she was going to suggest that we get married, and I wanted to act in such a way that would keep you from accepting that proposal."

"You were successful. Or at least, successful in making me think twice before deciding to make a lifetime commitment, but even if you'd been the nicest person I'd ever met, I probably wouldn't be super interested in making a commitment like that."

"Yeah. When I was in the Air Force, it seemed like women left their husbands constantly. There was cheating going on everywhere, and...that makes life sound pretty bad. There were also good marriages. But it felt like there were far more bad ones."

"Yeah. I felt the same way in the corporate world. It was crazy the people who are having affairs. Married people. I didn't understand that."

"Yeah. I guess I experienced it firsthand, because my wife left me."

"Oh? You were married before?"

He realized that if they were really going to go through with this, he was probably going to have to go through his life history. At least in enough detail so that she knew him. It was never wise to marry someone he really didn't know.

"Briefly. Less than three years." He wanted to be honest. He hated to make himself look bad, but he couldn't blame everything on Kylie.

"She cheated?"

"Yeah. I guess. I... I enlisted not long after we got married, and I guess I was pretty determined to be the best at what I did. And she got left behind. She was probably lonely. And while I wasn't as mean to her as I was to you yesterday, I wasn't considerate or kind. I was...selfish. Thinking about myself, wanting what was best for me. Which usually wasn't what was best for her too. I was a terrible husband. There. I said it. And she would be the first to totally agree with that. Because she said everything was my fault."

"I never made it to the altar, but I dated some losers. But I guess I was you, too. I was out for myself. Trying to see what I can get out of the relationship, instead of looking at what I could put in."

He hated this kind of conversation. Especially with someone he barely knew. And there was someplace they needed to be. "We can stand here and talk about it, or we can get going to the farmers market."

"I like that. Although, once we're there, it's usually pretty crazy busy, and we probably won't have much time to talk."

"Then maybe we can do that this evening."

She nodded, then gestured toward their vehicles. "I'd say you could ride with me, but I have my car filled up as full as I can get it. I don't really have room."

"That's fine. I'll follow you."

They walked in silence toward their vehicles but had to separate, because she'd come in behind him and had parked on the exact opposite side of the parking lot.

He smiled a little at the thought now, but he supposed it wasn't funny. After all, it was just another indication that he'd given himself an almost insurmountable task. Although Abrielle did not seem to be unreasonable. At least she was talking to him. Kylie would be giving him the silent treatment, probably for at least a week, maybe two, and Amanda would still be standing in the parking lot yelling at him, telling him how terrible he was.

Thinking about that, he knew if he was actually going to go through with this marriage thing, he was going to have to alter his thinking. He had allowed himself to think that all women were nasty double-crossers who blamed everything on men because it suited his narrative and worked for him.

If he wanted the ranch, though, he was going to have to figure out how to get along with Abrielle, and that would probably mean he needed to alter his view of women. Or at least of one woman in particular.

He honestly wasn't sure whether he even wanted to do that. Somewhere over the years, he'd decided that all the good women were married. And all that was left were women who were cheaters and double-crossers.

After all, if a man had a good woman, he'd do an awful lot to keep her. At least in theory. He'd seen marriages where men were so arrogant that they thought anything they did would be okay and truly did take advantage of good women.

There were also marriages that were the other way around.

He got into his truck and pulled out behind Abrielle. It was a beautiful spring day, the fields along the highway still greening up, and the sky was a pretty crystalline blue. It was much nicer to think about the landscape than it was to try to figure out relationships.

He did pay attention to where she was going, heading toward Rockerton, stopping before she got to the town limits. There, in a large parking lot of what looked to be a church, a whole crowd of people had gathered. The lot was full, and there were cars parked along the grass.

Abrielle drove by, slowing, and pulled in an alley just past the lot where she was able to drive up and turn around, parking, if not close, closer than she would have if she would have parked in the big one.

She got out and was back digging in her trunk by the time he parked his pickup and came over beside her.

"People start getting here at six o'clock in the morning, even though it doesn't officially open until eight. We're really late." She spoke without looking at him as she picked up a few bunches of lettuce and spinach that had fallen out of one of the boxes.

"I take it you're going to carry these over to a table?"

She didn't have any kind of thing to set up packed in her car that he could see.

"Yeah. Teagan and I share a table under the roof. It's in a prime area, and we split the cost. She'd been here for years and worked her way up to one of the prime locations. She shares it with me, although I'm not sure why."

"Because she likes you?" he offered as she picked the box up and handed it to him.

"I guess. Some people must." She gave him a look that was rather telling, and he wanted to murmur another apology, but he felt like he'd done nothing but apologize all day.

"Where do I take this?" he asked. The box wasn't heavy, but it was bulky.

"Hang on a second. Let me grab this and I'll show you. Teagan is already set up, I'm sure, and usually Deuce is here helping her."

"Deuce?"

"He's her best friend. He doesn't have a farm or anything, but they do everything together and have been doing the farmers market for a long time. It's like their Saturday friend thing."

"Deuce is a man?"

"Yes. He's handy too, because he usually lifts the things that are too heavy for us."

"This box isn't heavy; it's just bulky."

"I have some potatoes back there that are bulky and heavy."

"You grew potatoes already this year?" He didn't know much about vegetables, but he did know that North Dakota was still coming out of winter. It wasn't uncommon to see snow still on the ground even in May. He couldn't imagine someone had already grown something like potatoes, but maybe he was just showing his ignorance.

"No. We go to the auction and grab them Thursday nights."

"The produce auction?"

"Yeah. It can be pretty profitable, because they're sold in bulk at the auction, and then we sell them in smaller quantities here."

"I see." He hadn't considered the people who brought things to a farmers market might not have grown everything they sold themselves.

She picked up a box and started walking toward the tables.

"Aren't you going to close that?" he asked, referring to her trunk. "Or lock your car?"

She looked over her shoulder at him. "No. In all the years I've been here, I've never had anyone steal anything. I've even had people come back to me saying I didn't charge them for something or that their kid had taken an apple off my display and eaten it and they didn't realize, and they came back to pay for it."

"Really?" He could hardly imagine not locking his car and having people be so honest.

"Yeah. I know, it's kind of unbelievable if you've never been in a small town before. But, honestly, that's just the way it is. I'm not saying there aren't bad people. Because there are. It's just...a completely different mindset out here."

Even on the military base, he wouldn't dream of leaving his vehicle unlocked, even though he'd trust his life to most of the men there. And definitely most of the places he lived were not places where he'd leave his car unlocked—he thought she might possibly still have the keys in the ignition—while he walked away from it.

He still hadn't quite gotten over his shock as she wove her way through the crowds of people to an area that was covered with a roof. There was a building that looked slightly bigger than a shed that was completely enclosed with a door and windows further on but behind the two aisles that had shelter over them but were open at the sides. Like a carport.

"Abrielle! You made it. I take it the big meeting is over?" A smiling, dark-haired, blue-eyed woman met Abrielle and grabbed the box from her.

"Thanks. And yes."

"Did the big jerk get what he deserved?" the woman asked, lifting her brows, her smile just as bright as it had been when she saw Abrielle.

"The big jerk is behind me." Abrielle jerked her head behind her while the dark-haired woman's eyes widened, and her mouth made an O.

Chapter 9

The dark-haired woman looked at Smith. Her brows went even further up, and then she looked back at Abrielle. "You didn't tell me he was gorgeous."

"I didn't notice," Abrielle said, turning to grab the box from Smith.

He held onto it. "You did too. Last night in our bedroom, you couldn't take your eyes off me."

"It's not our bedroom. It's mine. And no, my eyes were glued to the ceiling. I certainly didn't have them on you."

"You guys were in a bedroom together? And… What's going on?" Teagan said, her grin only widening, as though she were expecting to get the juicy scoop.

"Let me gather the rest of the stuff up and bring it over. Then maybe I can tell you, where there aren't so many ears." Abrielle turned around and looked at him, indicating by her body language that he was the ears she was talking about.

"I know you have more stuff. Deuce just went to get us something to eat, or I'd send him back to give you a hand."

"It's okay. Smith came along and offered to help. Oh," Abrielle said, turning back around to her friend. "Teagan, this is Smith. Smith, this is Teagan, who I was telling you about."

Teagan grinned. "I wasn't sure whether I was going to get introduced or not."

"I'm just running behind today and have my head other places."

"She's trying to decide whether or not she's going to marry me," Smith said as Teagan held her hand out and he clasped it.

It felt like a wet fish in his hand though, at his words, which had obviously surprised her, as her mouth dropped open and her gaze went to her friend.

"Marry him? Have I missed something? You've known him for a while, and I just never met him? Or knew about him? Like you haven't mentioned him at all."

"No. I just met him yesterday."

"And she was in my bedroom last night," Smith couldn't keep from adding. He had to admit he did it just to see Abrielle's reaction, which was almost as good as he expected.

She pressed her lips together and shook her head. "I have to explain about that. That is not what it sounds like."

"But she is thinking about marrying me. I guess she wanted to see what she was going to get."

"I had no desire to see anything. And in my defense, when I was in my bedroom," she emphasized the "my," "last night, I was not even dreaming that there would be a possibility of the two of us getting married."

"Something really interesting happened between the time of the whole bedroom scene and this morning at," Teagan looked at her wrist, "9:30."

"Yeah. Very interesting." Abrielle rolled her eyes. "We'll be back."

"All right. I will be waiting. Trust me. I will be eagerly waiting."

"Hey! How much are these bunches of spinach?"

Teagan waved a hand and then turned back to the customer who had just called for her. Abrielle turned and walked back to the car, and Smith fell into step beside her.

"You don't have to tell everyone that we're thinking about getting married."

"Why not? Next week this time, we could be married." He emphasized the "be." Although he wasn't sure why he was even talking that way.

Just yesterday morning, if someone had asked him if he would ever get married again, his answer would have been a resounding no way. He didn't even like women. And yesterday afternoon, the woman who was walking beside him right now had been his least favorite woman in the entire world. Now, he could seriously be married to her next week this time.

"If we decide to get married, it's not like she's going to grab a preacher and have us say the vows that day. Surely not." She spoke like she knew exactly what she was talking about, except the last two words sounded more like a question than a statement.

"If I know my Aunt April, and I think I do, it was against her better judgment to let us 'live together,'" he used air quotes around the words "live together," "for a week. She's never been judgmental, but she's always been very particular about values and morals, the kinds of things our society doesn't think are important but that God clearly lays out as extremely important."

There was silence as they walked along a few more steps, almost back to her car, which, like she had said, was exactly where she had left it. The trunk up, still sitting there, everything undisturbed.

"You're right. Everything I know about Miss April says the exact same thing. But... That seems...fast."

"I need to make a decision fast. Maybe you're not in the same kind of situation, but I just had a bad experience with my business partner, and I lost everything. This farm was my last hope. That's the only reason I'm even considering this whole crazy idea."

Okay, as soon as those words were out of his mouth, he realized how they must sound to her. That she was his last-ditch hope, and he wouldn't consider her if he weren't desperate.

But he didn't know what to say to fix it. After all, he couldn't hardly backpedal and say it wasn't true. Because it was.

She didn't say anything as they reached the car and she bent over, pulling out another box, that one full of potatoes.

"I guess I'm the same. I have zero desire to get married. Absolutely none. But I guess I was hedging my bets on the farm. And I have a lot of things I've worked on, put a lot of time and effort and money into, and I was planning on seeing the money this year and in the next few years. I never dreamed Miss April would drop a bombshell like this on me."

She didn't exactly insult him the way he'd insulted her, but he understood what she was saying. The idea of marriage to him, or he thought she was saying to anyone, was distasteful, but she would suck it up if she had to.

"These are heavy."

"There should be fifty pounds in there. And I appreciate you carrying them."

"Sounds like Deuce would have done it if I weren't here."

"Yeah. He's great at helping us."

"So he really just hangs around because he doesn't have anything else to do?"

"He and Teagan are really great friends. They... They've always been friends. But that's just it. Nothing more."

He couldn't imagine having nothing else to do but hang out at a farmers market. If he were the romantic type, he would suspect that Deuce felt more for Teagan than just friendship, but he had his own problems, and there was no point in him trying to pretend that he had any idea of how things could work between a man and woman. He'd been a miserable failure every time he tried.

Abrielle was right about the box being heavy, but he still waited for her. This time, she closed the trunk, because they'd gotten all the boxes out of it, but she still didn't lock the car.

"Are you carrying a box of fifty pounds of potatoes?" he asked as he looked over. She had some kind of cover overtop the one that she was carrying, and he couldn't see.

"No. Mine isn't quite that heavy. I have some fruit in here, some late-season oranges, that I obviously did not grow on the farm, along with blueberries from Peru."

"Wow. I don't do too much shopping at farmers markets, in fact this is probably only the third time I've been to one, but I always assume the farmers grew the produce they brought."

"That's a good assumption. And it's usually true. But this is just a way to make a little money on the side. Also, because we have a prime location, it looks pretty bad if it's only half-full, and this time of year, I don't have a whole lot of things that I've grown on the farm to bring in."

He nodded, kind of understanding. He supposed the more things a person had on their table, the more likely they were to draw a crowd, and the more popular they looked.

"Sometimes Teagan's sisters bake things, especially late in the fall when the holidays are approaching. Pies and that type of thing. They even took orders last year and did pretty well. But I'm not sure I want to do that again. I have nightmares about spending weeks on end being in some kind of purgatory doing nothing but rolling out piecrust. It's enough to wake you up and not let you go back to sleep."

"I'll have to take your word on that one. Never had a nightmare like that." He had other kinds, like being a in hostage situation and not being able to get out of it. That would give him nightmares for a while. Not that he had been completely scared about losing his life, necessarily. It was the idea that he wouldn't be brave if the situation called for it. The idea of needing to step in front of someone else and take a bullet for them was nice in theory, but he hadn't been completely sure how he would actually act when the time came.

One positive thing that had come out of it was that it had banded him together with the men he'd been trapped with, and that turned into a very good thing. They'd been friends ever since.

It wasn't something he typically talked about.

They went back up. She nodded to people who called out to her. Obviously she knew a lot of the people and was familiar with them. She seemed to be well-liked as well. Maybe he should resent that, but it actually made him feel better. He didn't want to be contemplating spending his life with someone that no one cared for. That was probably a sign he wasn't making a good decision.

Of course, she probably wanted to see the same thing out of him.

A lot of the people he'd been friends with back in the Cities had sided with Kylie when things went down. It didn't matter how hard and long he defended himself, it was her word against his, because a lot of their agreements had been verbal. The ones that weren't were contracts he hadn't bothered to keep because he'd trusted her.

"Here. I'll take that and get them set up," a man said as they ducked under the roof behind where their stand was set up.

"You must be Deuce." Smith looked into the laughing eyes of a man who was almost as tall as he was and a little thicker across the chest. He definitely had a lot more laugh lines.

"Teagan, what did you tell this guy about me?" he called over his shoulder in lieu of an answer.

"Just the truth. That if he wants any fries, he needs to make sure he protects them from you, that if you asked to borrow his pocketknife, you won't give it back, and if you go over to his house on a Saturday afternoon, he won't be able to get you to stop watching golf on TV, even though you swear you hate golf and complain that it's the most boring thing you've ever seen. Oh, also, you claim that your feet don't stink, but they do. That's all." Teagan turned back to what she was doing.

The man turned back to Smith, shaking his head. "Lies. It's all lies. Especially the part about golf. Who could ever want to go watch that on TV? I mean, come on, what do they do besides stand around?"

"It's engrossing, isn't it?" Smith said casually.

"Yeah." Deuce lowered his voice so the ladies wouldn't hear. "I don't understand why it's so addicting."

"I usually start out watching the beginning, fall asleep during the middle, and wake up for the ending. It's nice noise in the background for a good afternoon nap."

"That's me too. Interesting. I guess you could be me in a former life, but that would be weird." He waved his elbow, since both hands were under the box of potatoes and they couldn't shake. "Good to meet you."

Smith didn't like too many men right off the bat. He liked to judge a fellow, get to know him a little, see if he would be someone he could depend on, trust, in a given situation, probably from his years in the Air Force, but he found himself liking Deuce immediately.

Of course, when he looked over and Deuce had set the potatoes down and taken the box of fruit from Abrielle, and they were laughing together, his feelings toward Deuce cooled immediately.

He wasn't sure why. It just showed that Abrielle liked Deuce, and the feeling was mutual. If they worked together as long as Abrielle had said, that was a good thing, not a bad one. Still, there was some kind of feeling, dark and a little heavy, that went through him at the sight of them laughing together.

It made him quiet as he and Abrielle walked back to her car one last time.

Deuce had offered to go, but Abrielle had told him to eat his fries while they were hot.

He didn't see either Teagan or Deuce eating much, because the line from their stand of people waiting to purchase, especially the fresh spinach and lettuce, was pretty long.

"How long did you say you guys have been doing this?"

"A couple of years. I've been living on the farm for just over two years, and that first year I was here, Teagan recommended that I plant some cool-weather crops and come to the farmers market with her. It kind of ballooned out from there."

"And it's profitable?" He hadn't considered using the ranch for that type of work. He had assumed he would raise cattle, if not just crops. He'd looked into it some and had a few ideas of the direction he wanted to go, but everything he wanted to do took money. This seemed like it might be something that would work, without a whole lot of initial investment.

"Yeah. It'll be even more so next year when my asparagus is finally ready to be harvested on a large scale. I've been taking a little here and there, but it really needs three years to be established. This will be the third."

"Asparagus?" He didn't think he had ever actually eaten asparagus. Maybe once. He kinda had the idea that it was gross.

"Yeah. People love it."

"I'm not sure I do."

"Maybe it just hasn't been cooked right. It's really good with butter and garlic."

"I can get on board with butter. Garlic might be okay too." He wasn't much of a cook. He could make mac and cheese from a box, and he was pretty good at throwing a frozen pizza in the oven, but he didn't typically cook himself vegetables. As in, he never cooked vegetables.

He was kind of sliding into the idea that this might be something he could end up doing. If it was, he might have to change his stance on the whole vegetable thing.

"You don't seem like the kind of person who cooks much."

Chapter 10

S mith could tell Abrielle's tone was conversational, not judgmental, as she opened the car door and grabbed another box,
along with a garbage bag. "Can you carry both of these? They're
not super heavy."

"I think so."

She handed both to him without comment, and he took them
silently.

She walked around to the passenger side and grabbed the box
from the front seat.

"Are you taking your keys and locking your car this time?"

"No. Not unless it's going to upset you. I suppose I can do it just
to keep the peace. But there's no need."

"Let me guess. You've been leaving the keys in your parked car
for two years and nothing's happened, so you assume that nothing
is going to happen?"

"Yeah. Basically. There's no reason to think something will."

He supposed his hostage situation was a little bit different, but
he'd gone to work every day at the hangar on base and assumed
that nothing was going to happen, until one day something did.

"It would make me feel better if you locked it and brought the
keys with you."

"But if I need anything from the car, if it's not locked, then I can
just send someone to go get it. If it is, I have to give them the keys,
and then I have to make sure I get them back. It's kind of a pain."

"How about you let me be in charge of the keys?"

She straightened, box in her arms, her elbow on the door ready to close it as she stared at him. "Is this a thing with you? Or is there a reason behind this?"

He paused, his mouth open. It was on the tip of his tongue to tell her about what had happened on base and how he'd been unexpectedly trapped, and while he hadn't died, it had shaped the way he thought. "I guess it's a thing with me. You never know when everything that you expect to happen turns into something you never expected. I just like to be prepared."

"And I like to trust people. Even when they don't deserve that trust. Even when I get surprised in an unpleasant way. I just like the idea that I live in a world where I don't have to look at people and think they're the enemy."

They stared at each other, him realizing that they had vastly different points of view and ideas of how the world worked, and that they approached life from two completely different directions.

That could be a problem if they were to get married. He would want to have the house locked up tight, and she would want to let everybody in, even if they were bound and determined to hurt them.

"Do you feed mice at your table?" he finally asked.

She stared at him, then her head kind of tilted and her lips ticked up. "Thinking that they turn into horsemen? Do I wave magic wands over pumpkins? Is that your next question?"

She had kind of misread what he had meant to say. But he laughed. Liking that she took it in a kind of whimsical turn. But realizing again that it showcased their differences.

"No, I meant, do you share anything with anything, even mice. Because we might be able to work through this whole *anybody can have my car, I'll just leave the keys in it so they can steal it easier* thing, but if you're going to invite creepy-crawlies into this whole *I share with everybody* thing, I'm not sure there's a compromise for us there."

Her brows went up. "Oh. I see. You're thinking about how different we are." She nodded as she used her elbow to shut the door, and they started walking back toward the farmers market.

"Yeah."

He noticed that she hadn't taken her keys and that she left the car unlocked. He wasn't sure if she did it on purpose, or if his comment had startled her to the point where she forgot about the keys and was thinking about their differences.

He kind of hoped it was the second, because if it was the first, and she deliberately left it unlocked after he asked her not to, he wasn't sure exactly what that meant, other than it felt like she didn't care what he wanted.

If she had specifically asked him to leave something locked or not locked, he hoped he would give her request deep consideration and not just go ahead and do whatever he wanted to, without thinking about her.

In his opinion, that's what you did when you were married. It wasn't just about yourself anymore, but it was about the two of you and what was best for both of you. Or, in this case, maybe not what was best—he clearly felt that locking the car was best for both of them—but what *worked* for both of them.

She had ignored his compromise of him handling the keys which effectively negated her argument that it was a pain for her to lock her car.

He tucked the information away. That was something he would have to think about if they were truly going to do this marriage of convenience. She needed to be able to compromise.

"To answer your question, no, I don't feed the mice. It is an old farmhouse, and I actually have traps and poison set out. I've seen several, and the less mice I see, the happier I am."

She stopped abruptly.

"Oh!" She looked over at him, then shrugged apologetically. "I'm sorry."

She turned and hurried back to the car. "I was going to take the keys, lock the car, and give them to you, and then you started talking about mice and carriages and pumpkins, and I totally forgot what we were saying."

He grinned. He couldn't help it. It was a big grin. A bigger grin than he had grinned for a really long time.

She set the box on top of her car, opened the door, grabbed the keys out of the ignition where she had left them, which made him shudder, then pushed the fob, locking the car and closing the door.

She turned around, holding them out. She paused, seeing the look on his face. "You don't have to look so triumphant."

"I'm not. Not triumphant, just…just happy that maybe we can compromise after all."

"Oh? I thought I was the one who had to worry about that. Aren't men supposed to be commanders and want everyone to do what they say?"

She looked around at him before taking her keys and putting them in his hand which was still holding the box.

"Maybe. I suppose that's my nature. But I understand that it's important to be able to compromise. I just wasn't sure if that was something you understood."

"All right. I know you don't mean that in a bad way. And I can see how you'd be concerned, because it looked like I was totally disregarding everything you said. Truly, you took me aback when you started talking about mice."

"Got it. If I want to distract her, I'll change the subject to rodents."

"Some rodents are cute. From a distance."

"Like chipmunks?"

"I don't think there are chipmunks in North Dakota. Although they look cute in pictures."

"In the Cities, you can actually walk up to squirrels in parks. They're really tame. They do have sharp-looking teeth."

They started walking back to the booth, and he thought it was kind of odd that he seemed to be able to talk to her about almost anything. Rodents, farmers markets, and he almost opened his mouth and spilled his guts about being a hostage. He hadn't been tempted to do that in a really long time.

She just felt so easy. Like he wasn't going to offend her. He supposed he'd gotten that idea the night before when, instead of getting angry at him, she'd laughed. He had gotten under her skin, he knew he had, but she hadn't allowed him to manipulate her emotions. That had impressed him.

"How long does this last?" he asked as they drew near to the back of the stand, having visions of being here until ten or eleven o'clock at night and thinking he probably should have asked before he volunteered.

"Usually, people are cleared out by the middle of the afternoon. The rush is always in the morning. The afternoon folks are looking for a bargain, and by then, I'm usually pretty willing to make a deal, just so I don't have to haul everything home."

"If you do, you shouldn't starve to death before next week."

"True." She didn't laugh, and he thought that maybe she had eaten a lot of the veggies she didn't sell. "A lot of the stuff won't be good to sell next week, so if I don't sell it today, I'm stuck. Blueberry pie, anyone?"

"Actually, that doesn't sound too bad. Maybe I'll have to grab a pack and hold them back."

"I'm not sure if I'm capable of making pies without having nightmares, but I suppose I could try."

"What if I told you that I would roll out the pie dough?"

"And you have experience in this?"

"It's rolling pie dough, not flying an airplane."

"You said you were in the Air Force. Have you flown?"

"I have my private pilot's license." It wasn't cheap to get, but that was the first question everyone seemed to want to know when they heard he was in the Air Force—what plane had he flown?

"So you fly, but it's a private license?"

"Yeah, you need to have so many hours in the air, that type of thing. I was in the Air Force, true, and I guess it's a common misconception to hear that and think anyone who was in the Air Force was also a pilot. There is a lot of personnel who go into supporting people in the air. I was one of those."

"I bet. People have to work on the planes, too. They do break down, right?"

"Everything breaks down. And yeah. A couple of the guys that I was close buddies with were mechanics. There are some body guys too. The plane gets dinged, and it needs to be patched up. Especially the ones that depend on really great aerodynamics."

"I can't imagine going that fast that close to the ground. It would freak me out. I'd have visions of myself plowing the airplane into the ground."

"It just takes a second or two. You're going so fast, you're flying so low, one little mistake is all it takes. It is a lot of pressure."

"Some people thrive under that though." She shrugged. "Not me. I like to think about pumpkins and princesses and carriages, and growing things too." She held the box in her hand and grinned at him, referencing the earlier conversation, and he returned her smile.

"The things I think about are slightly different, but yeah. I'm not too much into the high-pressure stuff either." The business that he'd started had been risk enough. Getting burned had only made it worse.

"Thanks a lot for helping me," she said as they walked to the back of the stand to set their boxes on the table behind where Deuce and Teagan were both helping customers.

"I bet those are our radishes, hang on a second," Teagan said, turning around and lifting her brows at Abrielle.

"He has them," she said, jerking her head at Smith.

He hadn't even realized what he was carrying. He set the box down and allowed Teagan to dig into it.

"If you want to help, you can. Most people will pay with cash, and you have to make change." She bit her lip. "I don't mean to insult you, but it's kind of a lost art. So many people that we've had help us have no idea how to do it. We don't have any fancy cash register. I just use the calculator that's on the counter, or if someone else is using it, I'll use my phone. Most of our customers can do the math in their heads, if you can believe that. They'll tell you if you make a mistake."

"I'm sure they will," he murmured, looking at the grandmotherly type ladies who were standing in line, some of them looking dour and serious, some of them chatting with each other, several of them holding the hands of little ones or with a surly-looking teen standing beside them.

There was a general atmosphere of congeniality, camaraderie, and it almost gave him the idea that he was dealing with his neighbors and friends, even though he most definitely wasn't.

It was a great atmosphere, one that felt safe and inclusive, even to a city boy like himself.

He would never have termed himself a city boy, but he'd been learning a lot of things he had no idea about until today and realized just how far away from the land he really was.

His eyes fell on the back of the woman who had pulled him, unintentionally, into this world. A world he didn't think he'd have any trouble loving. The woman? He wasn't so sure about.

Chapter 11

"Thank you, Mrs. McClure. And here's your change." Abrielle smiled as she put $0.52 into the old lady's outstretched hand, then lifted up the five pounds of potatoes she had bought. "I can carry these to your car if you'd like me to," she said, moving to go around the stand.

Deuce was already carrying produce for another lady, and Teagan was in the middle of a transaction.

"I can do it," Smith said from behind her. He'd carried several dozen ladies' groceries so far, but she didn't know him well enough to ask him to do it as a matter of course. It was hard to tell what he was thinking about the whole day in general and her in particular.

She'd been discouraged and depressed after meeting with Miss April in the morning. She had no desire to get married, and the idea of getting married to Smith was repulsive. Especially after the way he'd acted last night.

But today he had been a completely different person.

Not different, just...not deliberately trying to make her mad. She could see that had been what he was doing the night before. She was glad she hadn't allowed him to get to her. It was less embarrassing. After all, when she found out he was deliberately doing it, it was nice to know she hadn't fallen for it.

"Thank you," she murmured, lifting the bag up and handing it to him.

Their fingers brushed as he took it from her, and she deliberately did not look at him. She kind of thought he might be doing it on purpose, but why? To see if she'd react? He wasn't trying to make her angry anymore. So why would he deliberately brush her fingers with his?

She couldn't figure that out.

"Do you have a boyfriend, Abrielle?" Mrs. McClure perked up immediately when she saw Smith.

He was something to look at, too, she supposed, as men went. Not that she was going to fall for a handsome face. She was old enough to know that the way a man looked had nothing to do with the way he acted. And a lot of times, the more handsome he was, the more attention he'd gotten over the years, the more tendency he had to be stuck on himself and be arrogant, if not an outright jerk.

"No!"

"She does."

Her jaw dropped, as she had denied Mrs. McClure's accusation, while Smith had encouraged it at the same time.

That wasn't the first time today that someone had asked her if he was her boyfriend, and maybe this time, she said no a little bit more forcefully than what she needed to, but not forcefully enough to drown out his words.

Their disagreement only made Mrs. McClure laugh.

"Apparently, she doesn't know what you are. Maybe you should be more clear. Kiss her with the lights *on* tonight." Mrs. McClure winked. "If it's dark, she can't tell who you are."

Despite herself, Abrielle laughed. Mostly because she knew Mrs. McClure was harmless and just teasing them, but also because it had been dark last night when Smith had just strode into her house. And she really hadn't known who he was.

She hadn't found out his name until today.

She supposed she should have been upset that Smith was telling people, apparently, that he was her boyfriend. But when his twinkling eyes met hers over the whole kiss her in the light comment, she couldn't help but smile back at him.

If this relationship was going to work, they were going to have to compromise, but they could also have very distinct and separate areas for themselves. She felt that was key. There was going to be his stuff and her stuff. And then, if he wanted to walk through the house with his boots on, she wouldn't care. Because it would be his, and he would be responsible for cleaning up the messes he made.

At least it sounded good in her head.

Regardless, she could still enjoy herself with him. Even if they weren't going to have a conventional relationship. And if he wanted to call himself her boyfriend, she supposed it was okay. The very worst that was going to happen was over the next few weeks or even months, she was going to have to explain, possibly again and again, that he wasn't her boyfriend and never had been, they had just been thinking about getting married.

Well. Maybe she was going to have to have a talk with him. He was going to make her life unnecessarily complicated.

Although, if things didn't work out between them, she probably wouldn't be at the farmers market anymore, since she would lose the farm, so she wouldn't have to worry about explaining anything to anyone.

So there. He was her boyfriend if he wanted to be. She didn't care.

"He's fitting in really well. Can I say I'm impressed?" Teagan whispered in her ear as she waited for the teenager who had just purchased some lettuce and spinach for her grandmother to gather everything up and move to give room to the next person in line.

"I guess. I'm still not sold on him. He was pretty mean yesterday."

"What did he do?"

Abrielle pressed her lips together. Did she really want to bad-mouth him? If she told her friend all the terrible things he did, she knew Teagan would be on her side. But if she ended up married to him? Did she really want her friend to not like him?

Honesty was one thing, but keeping certain things private, especially things that really didn't make a difference, so that her friend wouldn't have a biased opinion against him, was probably the wiser choice.

The wise woman builds her house. That verse ran in her head. And another one: *A talebearer revealeth secrets: but he that is of a faithful spirit concealeth the matter.*

"I thought he was being mean, but he thought he was just convincing me not to marry him so that he would have the house to himself."

"How'd he get that idea?"

"He knew Miss April was going to tell us that we have to get married in order for both of us to have the farm. Otherwise, she's going to sell it."

"You're kidding!" Teagan looked equally impressed and horrified. "That's brilliant, and terrible."

"I know, right?"

"And you never met him before yesterday?"

"No. I didn't. And he didn't realize at first that if we didn't get married, she was going to sell the whole ranch to someone else. So, he set out to try to make me not like him. That's all."

"I see. And you're just having some trouble getting over it."

"I am. He's really not like that. At least, if I base my opinion on what he's done today, he's actually a nice guy."

"Anyone who can be patient with these ladies, take their teasing, and give it back to them the way he has, kindly and gently but still be funny...he's a keeper."

"I guess I'm more concerned about whether or not he's honest."

"Yeah. That's important." Teagan put a hand on her shoulder and looked into her eyes. She understood that, after having someone lie to her, it was hard for her to trust again. It was far easier to just write off men in general and not want to have anything to do with them.

"We'll have to talk more later," Abrielle said as they both turned back to the counter. The crowds were slowing down and thinning out, but they were still busy.

She had been blessed that Teagan had offered to share the space. If she had been starting out her own, she wouldn't have had nearly as good of a spot. But she tried to pay back Teagan by helping her as much as she could; the produce and crafts she brought complemented the baked goods and plants that Teagan sold.

More hours slipped by, and they had sold out of almost everything by the time the crowd thinned out and they started packing up to go.

"It's later than usual. I'm going to miss golf."

"It's not going to be a big loss. You're not that interested in it anyway."

"I am too. I love watching it. You know that."

"You love sleeping through it. Basically, what you're saying is you're afraid you're going to miss your afternoon nap."

"And you would miss getting to watch me and also putting my hand in warm water and seeing if you can't get a reaction from me."

"It worked once."

"What worked?" Smith asked, and Abrielle cringed. He did not want to hear that story.

"If you have a friend, a true friend, they don't take advantage of you while you're sleeping," Deuce said, sounding very serious and cutting a glance over at Teagan, who, while she appeared to be trying to look sorry, was failing miserably.

"What happens when you put a sleeping person's hand in warm water?" Smith asked. "I thought I'd seen every trick in the book in the military, but this is one I hadn't heard of."

"I'd tell you to try it, but don't do it to Abrielle. Particularly if you guys are going to get married. It's something she might hold against you."

"I see."

"Please don't tell that story," Abrielle finally said, hoping that was all it would take for them to realize that if she was going to marry Smith, she wanted him to think her friends were normal. Or at least as normal as possible.

"Well, it's like this, Teagan and I were at the lake, and I had fallen asleep in the shade."

"Pretty much every story about Deuce and me includes the fact that he fell asleep somewhere in the middle of it," Teagan interrupted to add.

Deuce gave her a look but kept talking. "She wanted to test this thing that she had read online, that when you put someone's hand in warm water—"

"Would you please stop?" Abrielle said with a strained smile as she stepped between Teagan and Smith with a box of their leftovers. It did include a box of blueberries, so she said to him, "And if you would take this to the car? There's blueberries in there, and if we get home in time, we can make pie."

"I'll get to hear the rest of that story sometime, right?" Smith said as he took the box and moved away.

"Yeah. Sometime when someone's not around to stop me. It's a good story," Deuce said, laughing, while Teagan had a fake scowl on her face.

"We have to get together sometime this week and chat. I want to know how things go this evening. And if you think you may be changing your mind," Teagan said, giving Abrielle's shoulder a bump as she carried her own box, following Deuce to the other side where they had parked together.

Abrielle had a few more things to box up, then she followed Smith to the car. That was everything for her, and they could leave.

The idea of being home by herself with him made her a little nervous. Not because she was afraid anything was going to happen, just because...maybe because yesterday had been so bad, but also because she wasn't sure how to act.

Just be yourself.

Right. She knew that was what she needed to do, but the idea still made her nervous. Maybe because they were talking about marriage, and that idea really made her nervous.

But as she was walking to the car, she realized she really didn't need to be nervous at all.

Lord, please make it clear what I need to do. Whether this whole marriage thing is a good idea, or if You have a different direction in mind for me. Maybe I'm supposed to leave the farm. Maybe this is a sign that what I thought I was building here isn't what You would have for me. Make it clear. Please.

Her desire, for the last few years anyway, had been to try to do what God wanted her to do. She could see that the major mistakes she'd made in her life were because she had tried to push things that she wanted, without doing what God wanted her to do. Of course, she supposed there were always times where God deliberately led her into an issue, just so she could get the experience involved in going through that problem.

It wasn't like the Christian life was smooth sailing as long as she did whatever God wanted her to do.

A lot of times, He asked her to do hard things.

A marriage of convenience was definitely a hard thing.

Chapter 12

S mith woke up Sunday morning smiling.

The farmers market hadn't been bad at all. He wasn't always a people person, but he loved the atmosphere there. The way everyone seemed out to help each other, and how everyone seemed to know each other, too.

Then, they'd come home, and Abrielle had made a blueberry pie as she told him how to cook asparagus, and he also fried some bacon.

Maybe a supper of bacon, asparagus, and blueberry pie wasn't exactly conventional, but it had been good. Even the asparagus.

If he was going to sell it, he probably ought to learn to eat it.

He could only imagine that today was going to be better.

They'd talked a little bit before they'd gone their separate ways after supper about going to church together in the morning. She said they needed to leave by nine, and he was in plenty of time, since it was only 8:15.

As he got out of bed, he thought he could smell coffee.

Waking up to the smell of coffee, yeah. He could handle being married.

Ten minutes later, he was downstairs, trying not to scratch his head as he stood in the doorway of the kitchen.

Abrielle had a roll of tape in her hand. She had a line taped from the middle of the back door, then down through the center of the kitchen, dividing the table in two, and up the far wall. She had the chair on the far end of the table pulled toward one side and the chair on the near end pulled toward the other, so there was no tape dividing the chairs.

Basically what she'd done was divided the kitchen in two with tape.

She was on a chair, snapping the tape off of the far wall, when she looked up and smiled at him. "Good morning."

"It was a good morning," he said, not meaning to be rude but wondering what in the world she was up to.

"I hope it still is. I woke up with an idea last night, and I was eager to try it, so I didn't talk to you about it, but we can discuss it if you need to."

"Okay." He eyed the kitchen again. The idea must have something to do with the tape.

"You look confused." The smile had not dimmed from her face, but her words weren't quite as chipper as they had been.

"Yeah. I guess I am. What's going on?"

"Well," she began, stepping down, flashing him a smile that was probably meant to reassure him, but at this point, he made a note that that was the smile that she used when she was trying to convince him that something that was not a good idea actually was. He had a feeling that if they got together, he was going to be seeing that smile a lot.

"I decided last night that one of the things that was going to bother me was if you came into the house with your boots on and tracked mud all through the house. So, what I decided we would do was we would split the house in two. That way we would know exactly what was yours and exactly what was mine. I won't be responsible if you make a mess, and of course you won't be responsible if I do, and therefore we won't be upset with each other."

He didn't say anything. But glanced around the kitchen again.

Finally, he said, "The refrigerator is on your side."

She didn't miss a beat. "You're right. So if you want something out of the refrigerator, you're going to have to ask me." She flashed him another one of those smiles that he had already catalogued as no good.

"And the stove is on mine."

"Exactly. So, if we're going to cook anything, you're going to have to do it." Her smile, if it were possible, got bigger.

He wasn't even sure what to say. Finally, he just said the thing that bothered him the most at the moment. "The biggest problem I see right now is that the coffee maker is on your side."

"I actually moved that."

"I noticed."

"Because I feel like it really needed to be on my side, because I suspected that since I was up earlier than you were this morning, I would continue to get up earlier, and everyone knows that the person who gets up earliest needs coffee the most."

"I think that's the other way around. Definitely, the coffee maker needs to be on my side." He paused. "And the refrigerator."

For the first time, she looked a little deflated. "I can hand you coffee." Her words were definitely less chipper.

"Or I could walk across the kitchen and make my own."

"This isn't going to work, is it?"

"We could try." He tried hard to say that convincingly. He didn't want to be known as someone who refused to compromise. After all, she had compromised yesterday when he had thrown a fit about the keys. But...that had been different.

"Really?" She perked back up immediately.

He forced the word out. "Yeah. If you are really stuck on this, we can...try...to make it work." He was almost positive that it wouldn't work. How could he come into the kitchen and not be able to go to the refrigerator? And how could she make supper if she didn't have access to the stove? "Am I supposed to cook all the time?" Because if he was, he was going to have to start watching a lot of YouTube videos. Or else invest, quite heavily, in boxed mac and cheese.

"No. Of course not."

"So then you're going to be on my side to use the stove?"

"Well, the microwave is on my side."

"Maybe we should switch sides."

"I don't want to do that, because the exit to the kitchen is on your side, and if you are over here, then you're going to have to walk across my side in order to get out, and if you're tracking mud, it's going to be on my side, then I'm going to have to sweep it up, and I'll be irritated."

"How about we just agree that if I make a mess, I clean it up?"

"Immediately?"

"Well, within reason. Maybe within twenty-four hours?" He had no idea if that was reasonable or not. But he didn't usually make huge messes. "Just for the record, I usually take my boots off before I come in. I left them on deliberately the day before yesterday because I wanted to annoy you. You do know that, right?"

"Yes," she said, her head going down. She bit her lip. "And you were successful. That's the problem. I hate being annoyed."

"I couldn't tell. You seemed pretty happy."

"Well, that's because I told myself that I wasn't going to allow you to manipulate me into not being happy when I wanted to be happy rather than being annoyed, but it takes a lot of work, and I'd rather just be happy, instead of fighting to be happy, if that makes sense?"

"I think it might. But I'll have to think about it." There were a lot of happys in there.

"Okay," she said, reaching for a coffee cup. "Can I pour you a cup of coffee?"

"I'd appreciate that."

He wanted to go over and get his own coffee, but he supposed that would be showing that he wasn't willing to work with her after she had been willing to work with him. And she was offering to share.

It wasn't like she was being mean.

He was pretty sure she would come around and see this whole kitchen dividing thing was probably not the best idea she'd ever had.

"How do you take it?"

"Black is fine."

She poured it, and he was careful not to step over the line but to stand right next to it as she walked over and handed it to him.

"Thank you."

"Thank you. And thank you for not yelling at me over my idea of dividing the kitchen. I think you're right. It's not going to work."

She walked to the wall where she had been standing when he came in, got up on the chair that she hadn't put away, and started peeling the tape back off.

"I'm sorry you felt like you had to do this. That's really my fault."

"No. It's not. It's just me trying to make boundaries so I'm not giving away too much. I have a tendency to jump into things with my whole self, rather than going in a little bit at a time, which would often be smarter."

"Marriage isn't really something you can go into a little bit at a time. You're either in or not. If we have to have a marriage where we need to have tape down the middle of the kitchen, we probably ought to rethink whether or not we should actually do it." He hadn't thought about that until the words were coming out of his mouth, but it made sense. If they couldn't figure out how to get along in the next week, the best idea was probably not going to be to divide the kitchen and get married anyway.

"I know. I guess... I'm scared."

"I've been praying about it, but I don't really have an answer."

"That's it. Same. And that scares me. I want God to tell me right now, like say, 'this is what you need to do.' Then I'll happily do it. The problem is, He hasn't. And I'm afraid of making a wrong choice."

"And it's a pretty big wrong choice."

"Exactly."

"Well, this is not in any way intended to influence any decision that you want to make. After all, I feel like both of us need to feel like God wants us to do it in order for us to do it, but we didn't really talk about the bedroom yesterday. I'm sorry I took it over. You know why. You can have it back."

Her surprised look said she appreciated his offer. "I wondered what I was going to do. I had a load of laundry in the dryer, so I'm not running around naked, but I was going to have to go into that room and get some clothes if we didn't figure something out."

"You weren't thinking that tape was going to solve that problem?" he asked, and she laughed.

"I suppose, if we think about it, we can figure out a way to make it."

"My granddad duct-taped everything. Including us boys on occasion."

"You have brothers?"

"One. An older brother. He was six years older than me and was killed in an aerial training accident while stationed in Germany."

"Oh. I'm sorry." Her face scrunched up. There was no doubt she really was sorry.

"It's okay. It was a while ago."

It still hurt. It probably always would. He had idolized and looked up to his brother. And his death had hit the whole family hard. His dad died of cancer two years after that, and his mom hadn't been the same.

"So…your brother died in an airplane accident, and that made you decide to join the Air Force?" She tilted her head, and there was true confusion on her face. She wasn't asking to be insensitive or mean.

"It's kind of weird how a man's mind works, isn't it? I guess I felt like it would be some kind of tribute to him. But yeah, the way you said it, it doesn't make much sense. Although, joining the Air Force was probably one of the best decisions of my life. Getting out of it was probably the second best."

She laughed, as he had intended. Although, he was serious about that. He learned a lot of things in the Air Force that he really needed in order to mature and grow up. But the military life was not for him.

"How many years have you been out?"

"Six. I enlisted for three, signed up for three more. I've been out for six."

"But you decided not to fly planes? Or is that something you don't get a choice about?"

"I enlisted thinking I wanted to. That was actually the reason I have my private pilot's license. Because of my brother. He helped me get it. By the time I enlisted, I had it, but once he died, I guess I kinda lost my love of flying, and I also figured it would be more practical to learn to work on them. So that's what I did. You don't have a whole lot of flexibility, but you do get to make a few choices."

She nodded, and he didn't go into more detail. It was impossible for anyone to really truly understand how the government worked, and the Air Force was probably no exception.

He just knew he'd made some of the best friends of his life there and had some of the best, and worst, experiences there, too.

"I guess sometime we probably ought to talk about...relationships." She fingered the rim of her coffee cup. "I know you said you were married before, and I was engaged. And while I'm not super thrilled about talking about it, if we're seriously thinking about getting married, there are probably some things you want to know about me."

Yeah. He definitely didn't want to go there. He had no desire to talk about his past relationships with anyone. But he supposed she was right. She deserved to know, and he was maybe a little curious about hers. After all, if she had been engaged to someone and backed out, he probably should know. Especially if she was the kind of person who got cold feet.

"I guess I feel like there will be plenty of time to do that this week. I assume you're going to be working in your garden a good bit?"

"Yeah. Thursday night, we have the produce sale. Usually Teagan and I go to that, but I can tell her that you and I want to go this week. She'll understand."

"I don't want to come between you and your friends."

"You won't." She said that casually, like she'd find a place to fit him into her life. He wasn't sure whether he appreciated that or not.

He felt like it shouldn't be her fitting him into her life, it should be her fitting her life around him, but that would be the way it would be within a normal marriage. Where two people wanted to be together so much that they adjusted their lives to accommodate the other one, maybe not accommodate, but he wasn't quite sure what word he was looking for.

Where they adjusted their life so the other person was the most important thing, the keystone around which their life ran. Assuming their entire life was built on the foundation of serving God.

That was in an ideal world. He was mature enough to know that most of the time, real life wasn't ideal.

"If you don't mind, I need to go into your room to grab some things to wear to church."

"It's your room. And I don't mind at all. It won't take me but a couple of minutes to gather my stuff up, and I'll move into the other room with a bed, which you said there is only one?"

"Yeah." She said it like she was preoccupied, and maybe the thought had popped into her head the same time it had popped into his.

Once they were married, they were going to have to figure out what they were going to do about bedrooms.

That seemed like a pretty important thing to him.

And honestly, while he didn't want to have separate bedrooms from his wife for the rest of his life, he wasn't sure he was ready to share a room with a complete stranger.

He set his coffee cup down on the table, and they started for the doorway at the same time.

He stopped, remembering their last awkward encounter in the bedroom. "I'll let you go first. I'll wait."

"I won't be long. I promise."

"You don't strike me as one of those women that take forever to get ready."

"No. I hope that's not a problem. Sometimes the women who take forever to get ready look pretty good whenever they actually are ready."

"And it's a bit of a shock whenever you see how they look when they're not ready." Maybe he shouldn't have said that, but Abrielle laughed, and he smiled back at her.

The morning hadn't gone too bad. If they could get through this awkward shifting of the bedrooms, and they'd managed to navigate the whole tape thing, and she'd seen things his way. The least he could do was offer to move back out of her bedroom.

Maybe he should offer to wash the sheets too.

"Abrielle?" he called, and he heard her feet pause on the steps.

"Yeah?"

"I'll wash the sheets this afternoon."

There was silence for a bit, and he couldn't help it, but he held his breath.

"I'll bring them down with me."

"Sounds good."

He wasn't quite sure whether she agreed to him washing the sheets, or whether she had just said she was going to do it herself, but either way, she wasn't resenting the fact that he had slept in her bed, and he was doing at least a little bit to make it up to her.

Chapter 13

"I saw him on the street on Friday," Sorrell said, looking at her friend Toni, who was nine, the same age as her. "Before the wedding. He went into the diner, and he talked to his friends, but he's new in town and I thought he might work for your mom or my mom." Sorrell kept her voice down. She didn't want anyone in the churchyard to overhear them.

After all, it was socially acceptable for adults to play matchmakers, but it wasn't socially acceptable for eight- and nine-year-olds to do so. Even if they were the ones who had moms who needed husbands.

"Merritt, you can't say anything, okay?" Sorrell looked at her little sister. Even though Merritt was only one year younger than Sorrell, everyone knew nine-year-olds were much more mature than eight-year-olds.

Merritt nodded solemnly. She was the quietest of the three of them. But that was to be expected, because she was the youngest too. Everyone knew that the youngest didn't have as much to say as the oldest did.

"Are we going to try to match them up?" Toni asked, her voice even lower than Sorrell's had been.

"We're going to think about it. He's definitely one that I think Mom would fall for. Although, she looked right at him and didn't seem to think anything about it." Sorrell lifted warning brows. After all, their mom needed to show some interest in order for them to be able to match her with anyone. "Mom keeps saying that she's too busy for a man. She doesn't understand that I want a dad."

"It's okay. We're going to get this figured out." Toni patted Sorrell's shoulder. Sorrell had more memories of their dad than what Toni did, and she missed hers more.

Toni, on the other hand, never knew her father and sometimes wasn't sure whether she actually wanted a dad or not. She just knew her mom was lonely. And a man would fix that. But it had to be the right man.

"Good morning, girls!"

Sorrell stepped back as Miss Abrielle came up to them on the sidewalk.

Her heart sank as she saw who was walking beside her.

It didn't sink too far, because Miss Abrielle was a really nice lady. She was always smiling, and she always talked to them. Some adults didn't. Or some adults treated them like they were little girls, when everyone knew that eight- and nine-year-olds were practically adults.

"Good morning, Miss Abrielle." Sorrell looked at the man standing beside her.

Miss Abrielle either took the hint or was planning on introducing him anyway. "I wanted you to meet my friend—"

"Boyfriend," the man interjected, and with that, Sorrell's heart really did sink.

"His name is Mr. Smith. And I think he's going to be here in Sweet Water for a while."

They all dutifully welcomed Mr. Smith, and then as Abrielle and Mr. Smith walked away, they looked at each other.

"That was the man. She already snatched him up."

"Should we try to break them up?" Toni asked, sounding a little too eager.

"We like Miss Abrielle."

"I know. I like her, but I like my mom more. And he was handsome."

"He was dreamy," Merritt said with an eight-year-old smile.

"He's taken. That means you don't look at him and think he's dreamy," Toni reprimanded her, like she was her own sister, which she practically was. They went everywhere together and did everything together, especially in the summer when school was out.

Even though there was a big difference between eight-year-olds and nine-year-olds, Merritt was very mature for an eight-year-old, and plus, it was nicer to have two people to play with rather than just one.

"We need to be faster. I saw him on Friday, and he's been snatched up by Sunday. When a new man comes into town, we have to jump that day." Sorrell, never one to sit around and bemoan her losses, knew that was the only way. They had to make a move, as fast as they could, as soon as they saw a new man in town. That was the only way her mother would ever get married.

"I agree. We need to come up with some kind of signal, that way when one of us sees a new man, we'll signal to the other ones, and then we have to figure out a way to trap him, preferably with one of our moms, and get them to marry each other before someone else comes in and snaps him up."

That was the thing that Sorrell liked about Toni. She figured things out really fast. It wasn't hard to get her on board with their new plan. A man comes to town, they kidnap him, tie him up with their mother, and make them get married. Somehow.

It worked in the movies anyway. It should work for them. They just needed to find the right man.

Chapter 14

"**B**oyfriend?" Abrielle gave Smith the side-eye as they walked away from the group of little girls. They were sweet girls, and Abrielle always tried to go out of her way to say something to them. All of them were living with single moms, and she knew what that was like. She knew what it was like to be a little girl who just wanted the attention of more mature ladies.

At least she had craved it when she was little. Always wanting them to acknowledge her, talk to her like she was an adult, and she remembered how good it felt when they did.

She loved that she was able to do that now that she was older.

Beside her, Smith shifted uneasily, shoving one hand in his pocket and running the other over his hair, which he had combed that morning, using water to get the pieces in the back that always stood up to stay down.

He left his cowboy hat home. There hadn't been too many times when he had worn it—the night he'd arrived being one—and she had to admit he looked just as good without it as he did with it.

But, boyfriend?

"We're thinking about getting married, next Saturday. It probably wouldn't hurt to let people know I'm your boyfriend today. That's only six days away."

What he said made sense, but it still shook her. Not necessarily the idea that he could be her boyfriend, although she wasn't sure she was ready to announce that at church. But husband. In less than a week.

It seemed fast, but wasn't that what a marriage of convenience was?

"I thought we hadn't decided what we were going to do?"

And if they decided not to get married, it was going to be difficult to explain to everyone why he was no longer with her.

Her words weren't accusatory, and she wasn't upset, not really. Maybe she should be because he had done it without asking her, but she understood that he wasn't trying to get away with anything or upset her. It was silly to get upset about it, even if she felt maybe they should have talked about announcing it at church today.

Before she could say that, he said, "I'm sorry. I guess that's something I should have talked to you about. I never even thought about it. I just thought I was doing something good."

She shook her head. "It's done now. And I'm not going to make you take it back. It might work out okay."

Or it might not. But wasn't that part of being a couple? When someone made a decision, they went along with it, if they could?

It wasn't hurting her or anyone else.

"I'll try to do better."

She wasn't expecting him to say that, and it surprised her. "Thanks."

It would have been a different story if what he had done had been beneficial to someone else, and he had shoved her aside. Then she would have questioned, if not his motive, at least whether it was a good idea to go into an arrangement like a marriage of convenience with someone who put someone else first. Even if their marriage wasn't a real marriage, they needed to put each other before other people. Didn't they?

"What are you thinking? You still don't look happy." They hadn't quite made it into the church yet.

She had to admit she was impressed that he noticed. "I guess I'm thinking that if this ends up not working out, it's going to be awkward. But if it does work out, I suppose it will be awkward if people didn't know about you and me at all."

She wasn't sure she wanted to keep talking about it and was relieved when she saw Miss Charlene and Charlie, her new husband, who, ironically, had the same name as her late husband.

"I'd like to go talk to Miss Charlene if you don't mind," she said, looking over her shoulder at him.

He nodded and walked over with her.

"I think married life agrees with you," Abrielle said as she wrapped her arms around Miss Charlene.

"I think it does too," Miss Charlene replied as she hugged Abrielle back.

Abrielle waited for Smith to shake Charlie's hand before she gave him a hug as well.

His cheeks reddened a little, like he wasn't quite used to ladies hugging him, but he patted her back, maybe a little awkwardly, and mumbled something about it being a good day.

She kept herself from laughing, just because Charlie was so sweetly socially awkward. And perfect for Miss Charlene, who was most definitely not awkward, at least not around people.

Sometimes opposites truly did attract, when they had enough other things in common to glue them together.

"I've been hearing rumors," Miss Charlene said, looking between the two of them.

It wasn't exactly a secret in Sweet Water that Miss Charlene had been heading up the Piece Makers, who were matchmakers disguised as a ladies' quilting group.

Miss Charlene had semi-retired since she had gotten married, but it looked to Abrielle like she still kept her finger on things.

"Hi, Aunt Charlene!" Sorrell, who had just spoken with Abrielle not that long ago, went running by with her friend and her sister.

"I didn't realize you were her aunt," Abrielle said, surprised. She thought she knew all the family connections in Sweet Water.

Although, the town had been growing, and maybe she lost track of a few people.

And she'd only been there two years. She certainly hadn't had time to learn how everyone was related to everyone else.

"The family connection is rather distant, and I'm not exactly her aunt. Maybe a distant cousin. But of all my relatives, Sorrell reminds me the most of myself." Miss Charlene's eyes were thoughtful, but Abrielle also thought they might be a little bit devious. She wondered what in the world Miss Charlene could be thinking in regards to Sorrell.

She wasn't going to find out today, since Miss Charlene didn't give her a chance to ask.

"Are you going to tell me if the rumors are true?"

"That I'm her boyfriend?" Smith said, his word a little bit more hesitant than it had been earlier, almost as though he was afraid of upsetting her.

It made Abrielle feel guilty, that she caused him to be a little bit insecure. She shouldn't have questioned him. If she had time to think about it, she wouldn't have. She needed to learn to think before she spoke. There was nothing wrong with what he had said, and he was right that it might be a good idea to just get people used to the idea, because next week they could be married.

"Well, that could be it. I didn't hear the word boyfriend. I heard the word marriage." Miss Charlene looked steadily at Smith, ignoring the people who were milling around them.

He nodded slowly, but Miss Charlene didn't look away, and maybe he felt compelled to speak. "We're thinking about it."

Miss Charlene's brows went up just a bit as she looked back over at Abrielle. "Still thinking?"

Abrielle nodded.

"I had heard 'marriage of convenience.' I suppose, marriage is definitely not something you want to go into without thinking. But in a case of a marriage of convenience, you consider the other person's character, what type of person they are, if they have honesty and integrity and character. And if they do, then you go with that. And you ignore the idea of needing to have a certain type of feeling."

"I think we know that. I think I made a bad first impression. Maybe not a lack of character, but a lack of manners."

Abrielle blinked. She wasn't expecting him to admit that. Not in public. And not to someone like Miss Charlene, who, while she was very sweet and nice, was also quite astute and was not afraid to speak her mind. From his short experience with her, she would dress him down if he needed it.

"Women like manners. They don't like to think that they're living in a barn with someone who doesn't know how to control his bodily functions."

She had to give Smith credit, because he laughed at that. Abrielle did too.

"That hasn't been an issue. Not yet anyway."

If Abrielle had to guess, she'd say that underneath his tan, Smith was turning red.

"I have the same bodily functions." Abrielle didn't know why she was jumping to his defense, but she felt like she needed to.

"Thanks for telling me. I hadn't suspected." Charlene's words held more than a little dribble of sarcasm.

Poor Charlie stood beside her, his face beet red on either side of his beard, and his expression saying he really wanted to go into the church and sit down and bury his nose in a hymnal.

Miss Charlene held tight to his arm, almost as though she suspected that was what he was thinking about doing.

"I didn't pass gas at the table, if that's what we're talking about here." Smith somehow managed not to sound ridiculous when he said that.

"And that's not something I would get terribly upset about, if it did happen." There she went again, running her mouth, just to try to make him feel better, and she wasn't sure whether she was making the situation better or worse.

"Really?" Smith looked over at her, surprise on his face.

"I suppose I might get upset if you had some kind of farting contest at the table, but since a contest would need to include two people, and you wouldn't be able to engage me in such a thing, even if we weren't sitting at the dinner table, it's not something that's going to be a problem."

"Not until you have children. I wouldn't put it past a man to engage his children, boys or girls, in a farting contest, as you so delicately put it, at the dinner table, and possibly make it a weekly tradition. Men aren't much on traditions, but I can see that becoming one a husband would hold to."

Abrielle didn't mean for her brows to shoot up to her forehead, but they had. Miss Charlene could be right. Did she wanted to sit at the supper table overseeing a farting contest between her husband and her children?

"Actually." Smith tilted his head. "It does kinda sound fun. I can see me...doing that, yeah."

He gave her a glance, as though he wasn't sure what she would say about that, but she got the feeling that he was just being honest.

The idea repulsed her, but Miss Charlene spoke before she could.

"Hold on a second, Abrielle." She put the hand that wasn't clutching Charlie's arm on Abrielle's forearm. "Think about this." She shot a glance at Smith. "You're not helping anything, I just wanted you to know that."

She looked back at Abrielle.

"What harm is there in a farting contest?" Miss Charlene hesitated over the word fart, like it wasn't one that was common to her vocabulary.

Abrielle could say that it wasn't one that was common to hers, either. She couldn't remember the last time she'd said that word. It probably wasn't one that she would want her children to say.

"Is there a verse in the Bible that you can quote that would lead you to believe that a farting contest would be unscriptural?" Miss Charlene paused, and despite herself, Abrielle considered her words. It wasn't something that the Bible had anything to say about, as far as she knew.

"That's what I thought. Think about this. Would you rather have a man who sits at the table and engages his children in fun and games, or would you rather have a man who sits at the table staring at his phone or, worse yet, doesn't even come to the table? A man who's glued to the TV set with a beer can in one hand and the remote in another? Or, even worse than that, a man who spends his evenings down at the bar, instead of with his family?"

All of those scenarios were absolutely worse in Abrielle's mind.

"Or you can have a man who's not interested in his children. A man who would cheat on you. A man who doesn't have character and integrity, isn't interested in raising children up in the nurture and admonition of the Lord."

"A farting contest is hardly raising a child up in the nurture and admonition of the Lord," Abrielle murmured, even though Miss Charlene's other words had penetrated and were working in her mind.

"Of course not. But the Bible doesn't say it's not okay to goof off. In fact, the Bible says a merry heart doeth good like a medicine. Would it be better for your family to play and have fun, or would you rather preside over the table with an iron hand, daring anyone to make any sound that wasn't first approved by you?"

When Miss Charlene said it like that, it sounded a little high-handed for her to have the idea that she should be in charge of what happened at the table. After all, the Bible was pretty clear about the man being the head of the family.

If she were dictating what happened at the table, she was hardly allowing him to lead.

Still, a farting contest at the dinner table didn't seem like something she wanted on a daily basis.

As though Miss Charlene could see she was wavering, she added, "Gas is a natural bodily function. It probably would be polite to not do it at the table, but I think sometimes we place an emphasis of importance on things that really aren't that important at all. Wouldn't it be better that you have a husband who teaches your children not to lie, to follow God with their whole heart, to discern truth from lies, to be in the world but not of it, and to not love the things of the world, but to love the things of God, and not worry about whether or not you have a farting contest at the table?"

Abrielle swallowed. She had been upset about the mud on the floor. She had not wanted to live with a man who would walk through the house with his boots on.

But if that man never did learn to take his boots off but raised her children the way Miss Charlene said, loving God, eschewing the world, seeking to bring people to the Lord, what did it matter whether her house had mud in it? What did it matter whether they passed gas at the table or not? That wasn't something that was biblical or necessary in order to live a good Christian life. It might be polite. It might be something that would be socially nice to do, but not elevated to the importance that she had placed on it.

She looked over at Smith. He had been the one who had been humble. He had been the one who had apologized, and rightfully so. He had been rude. She didn't want a man who was going to teach her children to be rude. But Miss Charlene was right. Smith really wasn't that kind of man.

"I'm sorry. She made me think that me getting upset about the mud that you had on your boots was really not all that important in the general scheme of things. After all, what's a little mud in the house when compared to eternity?"

"It was unkind of me to do. I... I don't know if I can promise that I'll never wear my boots in the house again. If there's an emergency, if I have to run in, I don't want to have made a promise I can't keep, but on regular days, the boots will always be off first before I step in."

She figured as much. His words didn't surprise her. She just nodded, feeling like she'd learned a lesson before she'd even stepped foot in the church. Maybe that was a good reason to come, to have fellowship with other believers, to be humble enough to take correction. Because sometimes she needed it.

"Good morning, ladies," a voice said, interrupting her contemplation. She hadn't even realized someone had walked up.

"Good morning, Gideon. It's good to see you here today," Miss Charlene said while Charlie greeted him as well.

"If you guys don't mind, we haven't talked to Smith in a bit, and we wanted to take him aside real quick before the service starts." Gideon had addressed his comments to the group, but he was looking at Abrielle.

"This is my girlfriend, Abrielle. Abrielle, Gideon was part of my crew in the Air Force. Behind him, Jonah was a member of my crew as well."

Abrielle greeted them both, shaking their hands, noting the grin on Gideon's face and the more sober tones of Jonah's expression.

"I'll be right back. If you go in and sit down, I'll find you, okay?" Smith raised his brows and didn't move until she nodded.

Maybe she would talk to a few people about him, just to be sure, but she thought that perhaps a marriage of convenience with him wouldn't be such a terrible idea after all.

Chapter 15

"**G**irlfriend?" Gideon asked as soon as they were out of earshot.

Smith supposed he should be happy that he waited that long. In his younger days, Gideon wasn't always known for being discreet.

"That's what I said."

"So the rumors are true?"

"What rumors?" He supposed it was pointless to play dumb, but he didn't want to admit to anything more than what he had to. He was already doing something really crazy.

"I heard that you were getting married."

"We heard marriage of convenience," Jonah clarified.

"I suppose you heard right then. Although, we haven't made a final decision, but that's what we're thinking."

"She's cute," Gideon said, as though he were paying her a big compliment.

"Fierce is more like it," Smith said, smiling to himself as he thought of her barreling down the sidewalk, totally determined to catch the cow she was chasing. And completely annoyed when he stepped in her way.

Maybe she wasn't ready to smile at that situation, but he sure was. She'd been impressive.

"Fierce?" Gideon asked, with lifted brows. He shot a glance back over his shoulder to where Abrielle was still talking to Miss Charlene.

Hopefully Miss Charlene was still encouraging Abrielle to overlook Smith's faults. He hadn't expected that from the older lady, and he appreciated it. Of course, she was right. And of course, Smith could apply that to himself.

He had been more concerned about driving Abrielle out than he had been in being kind. While that didn't really have anything to do with having a farting contest at the table, her words made him realize how many times he was more concerned about things that really didn't have any eternal value.

Like getting his way. He pushed and schemed and worked to get what he wanted, to keep himself from being inconvenienced, when what he was doing really wasn't important. It was other people, loving and serving and giving to them, that really mattered for eternity.

He didn't know if Miss Charlene's words had changed the way Abrielle thought about any farting contest, but they'd definitely encouraged him to be more mindful of what his focus was on and making sure that the things with eternal value were the things that were the most important to him.

"So your aunt outsmarted you after all," Gideon said with a sly smile.

"I don't know." Smith had to admit that maybe his aunt had had a good idea.

Although he wasn't completely sold on Abrielle, not yet anyway.

"You don't know? I thought you hated women?" Jonah narrowed his eyes, as though he were really curious as to what Smith was going to say.

"As women go, Abrielle has been the best one I've met in a long time." If ever. Maybe ever. He hadn't been around her much. But she hadn't been putting on a show for him either. She certainly hadn't been interested in impressing him. She had been just as uninterested in getting married as he was. But it seemed to him like her back was just as much against the wall as his.

"So now you're thinking you actually might want to get married?"

He nodded slowly, pondering this. When it came from his friend's mouth, the same friend that he'd told for years that all women wanted was to get what they could from him, in whatever way they had to, before they ditched him for something better when something better came along...the idea that maybe he had been wrong, that maybe he was going to do something he said he was never going to do again, was new and foreign and...it felt right.

"So if it's a marriage of convenience, why aren't you already married?" Jonah asked.

It was a reasonable question. Sort of like what Miss Charlene was saying. If they had decided to get married, they should do it.

"I made a bad impression. Walking around the house with my boots on, taking her bedroom on purpose, and making her sleep somewhere else, just being a general jerk."

"Somehow that's not hard for me to imagine, even though that's really not the way you are. It wouldn't take much for your natural antagonism toward women to come out." The humor had faded from Gideon's eyes, and he was completely serious.

Through the open church door, they could hear the strains of the piano and knew church was starting soon.

"So you've overcome that already?" Jonah asked, almost as though if Smith were going to say yes to that question, Jonah wanted to know what the secret was.

"I don't think so. Miss Charlene helped me a little, but I definitely dug myself a hole and jumped into it before I realized what an idiot I was being."

"Then you're going to have to make it up to her," Jonah said immediately. "That is, if you've decided that this is what you want. You don't have much time to change her mind."

"No. Only until the end of this week. Aunt April said we had until Saturday. If we decide to get married, the farm is ours. But if we don't, she's going to sell it to someone else who made an offer on it three weeks ago."

"Your aunt would take the farm from you?"

"It's her right. It's not mine. She's just giving it to me out of the goodness of her heart. And the fact that the house wasn't worth a whole lot. Or maybe she wants to keep it in the family. I don't know."

"Because she has money, and she doesn't need a farm, and it's just a liability to her. So she's happy to have someone else taking care of it." Gideon spoke as though he knew exactly what he was talking about.

"She would be okay with just keeping Abrielle on the farm, because that's what Abrielle's been doing. Taking care of the farm, paying the taxes, and doing upgrades when it's necessary."

"I see. So I wonder why she made the deal she did?"

"Not sure." But he had a sneaking suspicion that his aunt might have thought that Abrielle was a good woman and that Smith would never see that unless something drastic happened in his life that would force him to see that Abrielle was not the same kind of woman he was used to dealing with.

"If you think you want to get married, and you only have until Saturday to make the decision, Gideon's right, you really need to make it up to her this week. Women get upset, and sometimes it takes a while for them to get over it." Jonah didn't sound bitter, like he was holding it against the entire female gender, but like he had experience in knowing how easily offended women could be.

Except, Abrielle didn't seem to be like that. At least, she'd gotten upset, then gotten over it. For the most part. She even apologized for getting upset just a bit ago.

He was a little tempted to tell his friends that, but he almost thought they wouldn't believe him. After all, if they had tried to tell him that they had found a woman who would apologize for getting upset, he didn't think he would believe them.

In his experience, women didn't admit that they had been wrong. And they certainly didn't apologize. It was always the man's fault.

"Are you thinking about what we're saying, or are you ignoring us? Maybe you've decided that you aren't on board with the idea of getting married at all?" Gideon's glimmer of humor was back on his face.

"No. I think you're right. I don't know that Abrielle is even still mad at me, but I don't think it would hurt to do a little extra, if I'm hoping that she'll change her mind by Saturday."

"Although she's letting you call her your girlfriend. She must not be too upset with you."

"She did question me about that." It was true, she had. "What do you guys suggest I do to make it up to her?"

"Flowers, dinner, pretty words." Jonah shrugged. "All the stuff that women like."

Smith didn't say anything, but he looked over his friend's shoulder at the churchyard which was now mostly empty. Pretty much everyone had gone inside, and that's where he needed to go too.

He had enough experience with women to know that if he was late, she would be upset. Still, flowers just didn't seem like something Abrielle would really appreciate. He couldn't imagine her wanting dinner either.

Maybe it was him that lacked the imagination and not her who didn't want it.

"All women like those things?"

"I've never met one that didn't. My ex told me I didn't pay enough attention to her, didn't take her out enough, and never gave her flowers. Of course, that was amongst a bunch of other things she screamed in my face when she was walking out. But I caught that much anyway." Jonah shrugged, although the shadow on his face said the memory still hurt.

Smith would imagine that it had. Breakups weren't easy; divorce was a million times harder. "I better go. I don't want to be late. I know that'll make her mad."

"Why don't you just try being nice to her? You know, not treating her like she's your buddy, but like she's special. I think that'll work." Gideon spoke softly, his voice serious, his eyes a little sad, like he wished he could go back and do some things over again too.

Smith figured that was heartfelt advice and probably a good idea. After all, the Bible commanded people to be kind. That was basically what Gideon was saying. Be kind in a way she understood. Because sometimes a woman's idea of what kindness was was different than a man's.

"All right, guys, see you around. Although, probably not much this week."

He wasn't very good with pretty words, but he was good at working with his hands. Maybe there were a few things around the farm he can do.

Not necessarily improvements that he thought needed to be made, but improvements that would be something that would be beneficial to Abrielle.

He could be wrong, but he thought that was key. Making sure that whatever he did was something that she wanted and not something that he wanted her to want. Or something that he would want himself, so he would just assume that she wanted it too. He couldn't remember where he'd heard it, but he felt like that was a key toward understanding women. To not think like a man, but to pay attention to the things that she wanted, and not assume that she was just like him.

The idea was still a little new. That he might actually be going to try to woo a woman, with the thought of marrying her. And not thinking that women were the enemy.

He hoped he wasn't making a huge mistake, thinking that Abrielle was different than the women he knew.

Jonah snapped his fingers, making Smith pause as he went to walk in the church. "You should cook for her!" he said, as though the idea with the most exciting thing that anyone had ever thought of.

Smith had to admit that might be a good idea. Especially after she had been out working all day, the idea that someone would help her out, have something warm and good for her to eat, might be a good thing. It was something that he would appreciate, and he couldn't imagine that women, at least in this instance, were different. Everyone had to eat.

Plus, it hadn't escaped him that when she had taped down the kitchen, she made sure the stove was on his side. It had been an interesting position.

"The only problem is, I can't cook." Nothing more than boxed mac and cheese, and possibly hot dogs. As long as he could make them on the grill. He wouldn't know how to make them on the stove.

But he couldn't remember seeing a grill on Abrielle's porch. If he had money, he'd buy one, because he could at least do hamburgers and hot dogs.

"Miss Jane, who just bought the diner, is having a cooking class for—" Jonah stopped abruptly.

"A cooking class for?" Smith prompted when he didn't say anything.

"Old coots. She's having it for old coots, but anyone can go." Gideon's eyes laughed, and his lips twitched. "Even if you're not an old coot, but... I think you might be."

"I'm barely thirty. I'm not an old coot." He couldn't keep the irritation out of his voice. Thirty had seemed so old back when he was in high school and just enlisting in the Air Force. Now, it seemed young. At least, he felt young. Definitely not an old coot.

But he did want to know how to cook.

"Is it like a paid class or something you have to sign up for by a certain time?"

"No, I don't think so. She was doing it as a service to the bachelors and widowers that were in town. They hung out there anyway, so she decided she could help them because a lot of them had depended on their wives to cook for them and weren't eating very well since they died."

"That sounds like a good service," Smith said, meaning it. He supposed he wouldn't mind if someone had made the effort to try to teach him to cook at some point.

Of course, he couldn't expect that person to land in his lap. He had to do something.

"So anyone can just show up?"

"Yep. She'll take anyone, even you." Jonah winked, and they all started toward the church.

"What time does it start?"

"The sign on the door said one o'clock on Sunday afternoon."

Abrielle had said something about going to visit a friend that had cancer this afternoon after church. He hadn't known what he would do, probably visit with his friends, but maybe his time would be spent more profitably if he learned how to do something that would benefit her later this week.

"Are either of you two going?" he asked, just because the idea of going by himself was a little intimidating. But the idea of being able to cook, at least one meal, was almost worth it.

Plus, usually old guys were pretty happy to sit around and shoot the breeze, so he doubted he'd be the odd man out for long.

"Nope. I can cook well enough to get by, and Gideon can actually cook better." Jonah slapped Gideon on the shoulder.

"Eli cooks the best though."

"Is he coming?"

They both shrugged, and neither of them said anything. Probably they'd heard the rumors too that Eli had been dishonorably discharged.

He had been planning on making the Air Force his lifetime career and retiring from it.

Smith had no idea what happened, but he couldn't imagine that Eli had done anything dishonorable.

He shoved the thought aside, focusing on what he needed to do in order to get back into Abrielle's good graces. If he decided he didn't want to marry her, he'd have that option. But if he didn't do anything to woo her, he might not have a choice.

He liked choices.

Chapter 16

"**I**'m coming!" Cassie hurried to the door, coughing a bit into her arm.

She'd completed her last round of chemo earlier in the year, and her cancer had been declared cured, but that didn't keep her from wondering, every time she felt a twinge, every time she had a little cough, every time something didn't feel quite right...was the cancer back?

"Hello!" she said as she opened the door, laughing as her dog, Phylis, jumped around Abrielle's feet. "Phylis. Settle down. You know Abrielle."

"It's okay. She's so sweet." Abrielle bent down, and Phylis jumped into her arms.

Through the long days of chemo, the nights of sickness and fear, the days where she couldn't get off the couch and wondered what the point of life really was, her dog had been a constant reminder that somebody, something, needed her.

Even as she knew that God still had plans for her, because He hadn't taken her. She knew that, but Phylis was a daily reminder that someone truly needed her.

"Come on in," she said, opening the door wider.

"Teagan and Deuce will be here eventually," Abrielle said as she stepped inside. "I brought us drinks, if you'd like to sit on the porch?"

"I'd love it. I just started some plants out there last week." She led the way through her house toward the back door. "Teagan and

Deuce are always up to something," Cassie said with a smile. They were such good friends. It seemed like any day they would figure out that they actually liked each other for more than friends, but they hadn't so far.

Sometimes Cassie wished she had someone who seemed to like her as much as Deuce liked Teagan.

She didn't know why she was so stuck on Mav Stryker. He was never going to be a best friend the way Deuce was to Teagan. She should give up on him and find someone else.

The problem was, she had a tendency to get stuck on people. When she liked them, it was for life. No matter what they did.

"I saw you in church, but you ran in and out pretty fast," Abrielle said as they walked through the kitchen.

Cassie grabbed the vegetable tray she'd made the day before and opened the back door with her elbow. "I wasn't feeling very well. I have a bit of a cough, and I didn't want to give it to anyone."

"I didn't hear you coughing."

"I didn't. Not in church. But I sucked on a cough drop the whole time, and I wasn't there long." She allowed a smile to linger on her face. "I was there long enough to hear some rumors about you."

Cassie allowed the door to close behind her before she set the tray down on her white wicker stand and took the chair across from Abrielle.

When Teagan and Deuce came, they'd probably let themselves in or walk around the house. And they'd both sit on the steps. They'd done this often enough that everyone knew to just come in and be comfortable.

Cassie had to admit she looked forward to their Sunday afternoon chats. Working from home was awesome, because she could sleep in if she wanted to and just work a little extra in the evenings if that was what she wanted, and if she had a big project, she could work on the weekends or take a day off during the week if she felt like it. So much flexibility, but it did get lonely.

Being an introvert, she really didn't mind, but she often wondered if maybe that was why the Lord never saw fit to get her and Mav together. After all, Mav was outgoing, friendly, and a definite extrovert. He would never be happy hanging out in his house all day as she was.

Plus, his adventurous nature might have been a nice foil for her more conservative personality, but since her cancer, she really couldn't do all the things that he did, and she would just hold him back. Even if he had ever noticed her, which she would be fooling herself to think that he had.

Abrielle grabbed a carrot stick and shoved it in her mouth like she didn't want to talk about the rumors that had been swirling around the church.

So Cassie prompted her, "Something about a marriage of convenience?" She gave Abrielle a raised eyebrow. "And a boyfriend. Which, as one of your best friends, surprised me, since I knew nothing about it. Surely, if you had a boyfriend, I would know. Right?"

"In a normal world, you would have," Abrielle began. "But my life has not been normal. Not since I moved to Sweet Water anyway. For a small town, this place is just crazy."

"If you're talking about the pig—"

"Don't forget the Highlander steer, too. Everyone says he's mine, and I guess I do feed him the most."

"And you brought him to the wedding yesterday."

"True. But anyone could have done that."

"Exactly. You're the one who did. So, obviously the steer is yours."

"He doesn't live at my house, and I can't catch him long enough to get him to go."

"You caught him long enough to let kids pet him."

"I know. But when I turn my back, it's almost like he can read my mind. Like he knows I'm done, and he slipped away before I could get someone with a trailer to load him up."

"Are you trying to tell me that the steer is...smart? Because, even for a person who really is a cow person, that's a little unbelievable to me."

"I know. I love cows, but they're not exactly known for their intelligence. I suppose I'm giving him human characteristics, but it does seem like he somehow does know that he needs to slip away, or else he's going to be caught."

"Maybe he needs to be around people?" Cassie asked, and she couldn't keep the wistfulness out of her voice.

Mav was the kind of man who needed to be around people. She supposed it wasn't exactly complimentary to compare him to a cow, even a Highlander that she liked, but it was true. He wouldn't be happy tied down with her. And it would be tied down.

He would want a big family, lots of kids, and she wasn't even sure she could have kids. He'd want to be in the middle of everything, and she had to avoid anyone who looked like they might be sick. He'd want to do all kinds of dangerous things, and she'd come close enough to death that she didn't care if she ever stared it in the face again.

"You're thinking about something," Abrielle pried gently.

"Don't try to turn the subject onto me. We're talking about you and this mysterious boyfriend you have. Which, by the way, he was cute."

"Smith is definitely cute, but a lot of times, guys who look good are rotten inside. Where you can't see. Being the center of attention spoils them. Makes them think they're better than what they are, or maybe makes them rely on their looks rather than their character to attract women."

"Maybe that's not all the man's fault. After all, if women are attracted to a good-looking man and not to a good man's character, that's on us, not them."

"True." She thought again of Mav. He was good-looking, and she thought he had a good core as well. There were times where he'd been a little immature. Okay, when he was younger, a lot immature. But he had a great sense of humor and always made her laugh. Even if it was just her listening to him talk to someone else, since he'd never actually deliberately set out to make her laugh. He was always charming other people.

Charming. That was probably a good word for Mav.

Charming. A charming rascal.

Why in the world was she attracted to such a man? And so stuck on him that she couldn't seem to get herself to notice anyone else?

"But Miss Charlene seemed to think he is someone worth pursuing."

"Miss Charlene has a bit of a reputation for knowing when someone has character and integrity."

She had quite a reputation for matchmaking as well, although Cassie had never been on her list of people to match.

Not because she wasn't the correct age, but because who wanted to be matched to someone who could die at any moment?

That might be a bit of an exaggeration, but no one wanted to marry someone who was sick. Or who had a higher-than-normal chance of getting sick again.

She had accepted it and was mostly okay with it. Just, it made her a little sad that she would never be on the matchmaker's list.

"So is there really going to be a marriage of convenience?" Cassie tried to focus on the subject in hand. She wanted to be a good friend.

"Maybe. Miss April, who owns the ranch that I'm on," Cassie nodded, because she knew that, "has told us that she didn't want to take the ranch from me to give it to Smith, who is her nephew, but she also didn't want to not give it to Smith, because he's her nephew."

There were some repeating words in there, and Abrielle smiled as Cassie processed the facts.

"So?"

"So, the compromise that she came up with was to say that she would give it to both of us, but only if we got married. She is not okay with us living together, of course."

"Of course. So where is Smith staying now?"

"Actually, she gave us a week to stay on the farm together. She said that was all she could give us."

"You and Smith are staying together at the farmhouse?"

"Yeah." Abrielle grinned. "Actually, he slept in my bed last night."

"You gave him your bed?"

"No. He took it."

Abrielle launched into a story about Smith tracking mud through the house, and taking her bedroom, and doing it on purpose to try to make her not like him so she wouldn't want to marry him, all because he knew that his aunt was going to say that she wanted them to get married. What he didn't realize was that she was going to make it a contingency for either one of them getting the ranch.

"So it came back to bite him, which was a very fast-growing seed if you reap what you sow."

"Oh, you reap what you sow, all right. Sometimes it just takes a long time." That was true. And she believed it. But it was also true that sometimes she didn't feel like she would be around long enough to reap her harvest.

At least, in her life, God had to have things growing fast. Or maybe she'd reap in heaven. She supposed that was a distinct possibility and probably the best thing that could happen to anyone, even if it didn't feel like it at the time.

"You do. Sometimes...sometimes when the harvest takes a long time, it's hard to remember that. You know, how you're kind to someone for ages, and they're always mean, and you wonder if God's ever going to have you reaping what you sow?"

"I get that. But I think maybe He has a plan for that too. The longer we have to wait, the more our faith grows. And the more we have to cling to our faith and believe His promises."

"Either that, or we walk away from our faith. Lots of people do that too. They throw their hands up and give up on God."

"Maybe that's what He means about separating the wheat from the chaff? Who are the people that are going to trust Him, trust Him for a long time no matter what? And who are the people who are going to give up and walk away?"

"It's a good test, I guess."

"Yeah. I've often thought about Abraham and Sarah. They're held up in the Bible as an example of faith. We never think about it, but God promised them a son, and then how many years was it until they actually had one?"

"I forget. Decades, wasn't it?"

"I think so. Maybe twenty-five years? Anyway, if God gives me a verse, a verse that's a promise, somehow I think in my head that, okay, that's going to happen right away. But just like Abraham and Sarah waiting twenty-five years for Isaac, maybe God's given me a promise, and He wants to know if I'm going to believe Him for twenty-five years until it actually happens?"

"Wow. That's a good point. One I hadn't thought about before. I definitely think I would give up before twenty-five years, and I'm kind of ashamed to say it."

"Me too. But I do think that God wants to see if we're going to keep planting and watering and doing what we're supposed to do, trusting in His promises."

"Standing on the promises, right?"

"Great song. And a good reminder of what we're supposed to do."

They sat in silence for a bit, and then Cassie gently prodded Abrielle. "So you're not married? Have you decided to do that? You know. Those church rumors."

"He called me his girlfriend almost as soon as we set foot on the property. I suppose it took about five minutes before everyone in the church lot knew that I was walking in with a 'boyfriend.'" Abrielle used air quotes around the word "boyfriend."

"That's small towns. We all like to keep up with each other."

"I know. Not in a gossiping way, but in a way that shows that we care about each other. We can hardly help each other if we don't know what's going on in each other's lives."

"Yeah. I think that's one of the problems with society today, we're all so focused on our screen time that we don't know what's happening in real life around us."

"We don't understand the difference between gossip and caring."

"Possibly."

Gossip was talking about someone with malicious intent. Spreading information that may or may not be true, a lot like what passed for news nowadays. "News" was more gossip than trying to figure out whether someone was with a boyfriend or not.

"I think we just decided to spend the week maybe getting to know each other. After all, he didn't make the best first impression on me and... I didn't tell you, but kind of in retaliation, I divided the kitchen into halves and told him he was only allowed on his half."

"You're serious?" Cassie said, her mouth fully open despite herself.

"Yeah. It was short-lived, because the refrigerator was on my side and the stove was on his. It would be kind of hard to live like that."

"I'll say. What in the world were you thinking?"

"I was thinking I didn't want to allow him to make me angry. Because when someone makes you angry, they're controlling you.

And I wasn't going to allow him to control my emotions and how I felt. I guess I felt like I was being preemptive."

"In a..."

"Not very smart way. Go ahead. You can say it. It was dumb."

"Your words."

"But I know you agree."

They laughed together.

"So, yeah. I didn't make the best impression on him either. That was this morning, although so much has happened since then it feels like a long time ago."

Chapter 17

"**S**o this morning before church you divided your kitchen in half?" Cassie asked again in amazement.

"Yeah. You didn't look around the congregation at church and wonder what people did in the morning before they came?" Abrielle gave a self-depreciating smile. "That was my morning."

"I had a much calmer morning. I fed Phylis, ate some breakfast, and was deliberately late. And I don't have a marriage of convenience looming over the top of my head, either. I suppose your behavior can be excused because of that. That has to be a lot of pressure."

In a way, it would be kind of nice. Nice to have the choice taken away and then to just have to forge a life with someone that had been picked for a person.

She supposed she didn't want to move back to the time of arranged marriages, but there was something appealing about being matched up with someone and foregoing all the hassle of dating and trying to figure out if you were with your soulmate, or if there was someone else out there who was even more perfect for you.

Most people were looking for that perfect person because they didn't want to have to overlook faults and flaws in their partner, even though their partner was most assuredly going to have to overlook faults and flaws in them.

"Maybe on Saturday, I'll feel pressure, but right now, I don't. I just... I guess I want to keep the farm. I don't know what I'm going to do if I don't."

"You're great at growing things. I know that's not what your original job was, back when you worked in the corporate world, but you're good at it. You could find a job in a greenhouse or on a produce farm."

Abrielle nodded slowly. "I suppose you're right. I hated what I did in the corporate world. Hated working there. So much back-biting and cutthroat competition. I had some good friends, but it was just so stressful. And there were some really rotten people."

"Someone needs to be a light there. Maybe that's where God wants you?"

"Maybe."

"But He's given you this opportunity... Maybe that's what He wants? Maybe it's just crazy enough to be a situation that God wants to work out."

"I've wondered. I... I'm not as aghast about it as I was at first. Kind of getting used to the idea and it doesn't feel so terrible."

"I'll pray for you, that you have clarity. But it sounds to me like you're already thinking along those lines."

"I am. I don't want to do anything God doesn't want me to do. But sometimes He puts crazy things in front of us, just to test us and see if we'll trust Him. I was sure when I lost my job and came to the farm that that was exactly where He wanted me. And I'm starting to think that maybe He wanted me there, not just so I could grow and sell produce, but...so I could meet Smith."

"Maybe you'll end up falling in love with him?"

"Maybe. I don't really think that's as important as what Miss Charlene told me today. That he has character and integrity. And will keep his word. That's the important thing."

Cassie nodded. "I agree."

Again she wondered why she was still so stuck on Mav. Although, she believed he had character and integrity and would do what he said he would do. He just... Maybe he didn't seem that way to other people. But maybe she was deceiving herself, thinking she saw something that other people didn't see. Although Miss Charlene must have seen something, because she was willing to match him with someone, and she wouldn't have been willing if she hadn't thought he would keep his word.

"I think a marriage of convenience is kind of romantic." She tried not to sound dreamy, because it would be scary too. The whole idea of making a pledge of that magnitude to someone that she barely knew was definitely scary. But also... "Just the idea. Probably the reality is a little different."

"Probably. But... I know what you mean." Abrielle gave a little smile. "I didn't mind sitting beside him in church today. And, he's been considerate and sweet." She sighed. "What I need is to be sure that I'm doing whatever it is that God wants me to do, even if it's something that seems a little crazy."

"Guys! I'm sorry really!" Teagan came around the corner, and Cassie had to stifle a gasp.

Abrielle didn't stifle hers. She put a hand to her throat. "What happened?"

Teagan was covered in mud, completely covered in mud. And as she moved forward, Deuce came behind her. The only thing white on his entire body was his teeth when he smiled. Even they had a streak of mud on them.

Cassie started to stand. "I'll go get you some towels to clean up with."

"Don't worry about that. We're going to go take a dip in a water trough somewhere. But I wanted to come by and tell you that we're not going to be here today."

"What happened?" Cassie asked as she settled back in her chair. She supposed a water trough was probably what those two needed.

"Someone thought it would be a bright idea to catch the pig that's been running around Sweet Water." Teagan gave Deuce a look that lost some of its effectiveness because of the dirt on her face, although the whites of her eyes stood out in stark contrast to the mud on her cheeks and forehead.

"Whoa, whoa, whoa," Deuce said, holding both hands up. "I simply said someone should catch the pig." He emphasized "someone." "I didn't say it should be us."

"You strongly insinuated that it should be us, especially since the pig was right there." She emphasized the "right there," so much that Cassie actually craned her head to see if the pig really was right there.

"I might have strongly insinuated, but it was your job to say, 'no, Deuce, we don't want to chase the pig, because we're going to end up covered in mud.' And you didn't do your job."

"If that was my job, you should have said so. I thought my job was to say, 'yes, Deuce. Let's do whatever you say, Deuce.'"

"Well, that is normally your job, but that wasn't your job today. You need to know when these things change."

"You need to tell me when these things change."

"They change whenever they need to change, and you need to be ready to move with the program."

"I'm ready to move, in fact, we moved quite fast down the street, as I recall." Teagan sighed. "We did almost have him, didn't we?"

"Yeah. If it hadn't been for that spot where the plow truck got stuck in the parking lot and made a big rut, and you hadn't tripped—"

"Wait. I didn't trip over the rut. I tripped over you."

"Are you sure about that? I don't remember."

"You don't remember, because you were the one who tripped first."

"I'm pretty sure you're wrong about that."

"I'm sure someone has it on video. We'll have to find out, then we'll know exactly what happened."

"If there is no video, I'm gonna go on the record saying you tripped first. If there is a video, you might be right."

"You know I'm right!" Teagan said, smacking his arm.

Cassie just sat and watched with a smile on her face, the same as Abrielle. Those two were always so entertaining. They never acted their age when they were around each other, seeming to bring out the kid in each of them.

What fun it would be to have a friend like that, Cassie thought, for not the first time.

"I know no such thing. In this relationship, most of the time I'm right and most of the time you come around to my way of thinking, once your brain catches up to your mouth." Deuce winked at Cassie and Abrielle as Teagan put her hands on her hips.

"That's not the slightest bit true! You are the one that usually comes around to my way of thinking, although it usually takes you longer than a day, because your brain is super slow."

"It was definitely super slow today when you suggested we chase that pig. It's just now that I'm realizing that I should have said no."

"That's funny, because I realized I should have said no to you just before I fell into that big mud puddle."

"You had a hold of the pig, too. I don't understand why you let it get away."

"Because I was lying in mud!"

"It would have made it all worthwhile to get muddy if we had caught the pig. Now, since you let go of it, we're just muddy."

"At least I had my hands on it. That was more than you accomplished."

"That was because you shoved me out of the way and then tripped me."

"You have a really convoluted idea of what actually happened." She shook her head, in mock consternation, and looked up at

Cassie and Abrielle. "I'm going to go find a water trough to sit in. And if you mention this to anyone, make sure you tell the truth. He was the one who tripped me." She pointed to him and then herself to emphasize her words.

"Got it. Both of you are muddy, you both are arguing—nothing new there, and the pig is still running loose. Anything else, they can get from you." Abrielle laughed as she spoke.

"If you come back when you're cleaner, we'll feed you."

"He owes me a meal in the diner anyway. From yesterday when he—"

"No. You're the one who owes me a meal at the diner."

They were still arguing back and forth as they walked back around the side of the house.

"Those two are just too stinking cute," Abrielle said with a smile.

"I wonder when they're going to realize that they're perfect for each other?" Cassie knew she had a silly smile on her face, but she couldn't help it. She looked at Abrielle. "If I'm ever that oblivious, would you please say something to me?"

"Of course. I think maybe someone should say something to Teagan."

"I've mentioned it before, kind of casually, but she said that they have such a great friendship, she wouldn't want to ruin it trying to do anything else. And I guess I kind of get that."

"Me too. Sometimes when romantic relationships go sideways, you end up with no relationship at all. And what they have is so special. But..."

"They're never going to find a better person to be with than each other."

"Exactly."

Would anyone ever say that about her and someone else? She doubted it. Cancer had stolen a lot of things from her, and the opportunity to have a husband and family was almost certainly one of them.

"Maybe someday people will say that about you and Smith, that you're perfect for each other. And they'll have no idea that you met one week and married the next."

"Wouldn't that be ideal? But how often does life actually work that way?"

"I think a lot of times life works the way we determine it's going to."

She probably should listen to her own advice. After all, cancer only stole what she allowed it to. And anything she couldn't get back, she could replace with other, better things.

The important thing was her mindset. And what she believed. Because, if she lived her life thinking that she would have a lesser life because of cancer, it would almost certainly be true. But if she lived her life determined to only allow her cancer diagnosis to make her stronger, that would be true too.

"You know what, as I'm sitting here, I think you should go for it." She turned to Abrielle and lifted her brows, sincere and entirely sure of what she was saying. "I think it could end up being the best decision you ever make."

Chapter 18

S mith paused with his hand on the diner door, reading the sign.

> **Diner closed until six. Special today: Crockpot Cream Cheese Chicken Chili.**

A smaller sign said:

> **Cooking lessons one o'clock. Anyone welcome.**

Unsure as to whether this was the proper door to use or not, he tried it and found it was unlocked.

Taking a breath, trying not to internally roll his eyes over the things a man would apparently do for a woman, he walked in.

It wasn't even a woman he loved. Just a woman he wanted to marry. Crazy that they would not be the same thing.

What would it take for him to love Abrielle?

Somewhere in the back of his mind, he knew that he wasn't interested in all the tingly feelings kind of love. He wanted the real kind. The kind that lasted for a lifetime, as looks faded, skin sagged, and bodies expanded.

He didn't know how to give that kind of love or where to find it.

Maybe that was something he could learn.

"So we're going to start out with a—" The female voice cut off abruptly, and then she said, "I'm sorry, we're closed until six. But come back. It's going to be good today."

"I was here for the cooking lessons." He tried not to feel like an idiot as he said it, because he could clearly see three old and grizzled gray heads standing around a pretty young face, with hair pulled severely back and caught in a ponytail.

He must be older than the cook but decades younger than any of the other "students."

"Oh." There was a pause as the woman's tone conveyed her total shock, and her silence clearly said she wasn't sure what to do with him.

"If... I'm too young, it's okay. I can leave." He actually started to turn around, his hand reaching for the door, kicking himself for doing something this stupid, when her voice stopped him.

"No! I'm... I'm just so happy that someone else decided to come. I'm sorry. Come on back. I'll get you a hairnet."

He supposed the other fellows really didn't have any need for hairnets. Which is why they weren't wearing any.

"I have a religious exemption for hairnets," one of the fellas said with a wink.

"I do too," the next fella said.

"I'm allergic to milk, and the hairnets were probably made on equipment that might have touched milk at some point, so I couldn't wear one."

Smith glanced around the three men who were looking at him with absolutely serious expressions on their faces.

"Sometimes I swell up when I get stung by a bee," he said, kind of uncertainly.

"Oh," the woman said. "Then maybe you shouldn't wear one either. You might possibly have a latex allergy in addition to your bee allergy, and I don't want to have to stop the lesson to rush to the emergency room."

Smith's eyes narrowed. He looked around the room. There wasn't a hairnet in sight.

He almost opened his mouth to ask if the woman even had hairnets, but they all seemed so happy with their little deception that he hated to ruin it.

"If I come back for another lesson, I could shave my head." He would definitely fit in better if he were bald.

"Your hair is almost long enough to put in a ponytail," one of the men said.

"You'd need two. One for the top of your head and one for the bottom," the second man said, his bushy eyebrows the only thing on his head that might possibly need a hairnet, since the top of his head was as shiny as a glass Christmas ornament. "I'm Marshall, by the way." The man held out his hand.

"I was going to say we should have introductions," the woman said. "I'm Jane. I bought the diner not long ago, and I'm the one who's doing the cooking lessons."

Smith pulled his hand back away from Marshall's and grabbed a hold of Jane's proffered appendage. "I'm Smith. I just moved to Sweet Water."

"We all know you," the second man said. He held out his hand. "I'm Blaze. And I'm a little envious of all of your hair. If you shave it, I'll probably have to pluck out the last five strands of mine that are on top of my head, and I would really hate to do that. So, if you come again, please don't."

Smith laughed in spite of himself. "Maybe you could just cut a couple of inches off of them," he said, eyeing the five or six long strands of hair that lay on top of the man's head. He had them combed over to the side, so they stretched from the right side of his head all the way over to the other side and hung down by his ear.

"I hate to do that," Blaze said. "I don't want to discourage them and have them give up the ghost and fall out. They're all I have left."

Smith nodded solemnly, trying not to smile, since Blaze wasn't smiling.

"I'm Theodore M. Ranchell the Third," the last man said. "But everyone calls me Junior. You can too. I wouldn't know what to do if someone actually called me Theodore. I wouldn't recognize it, first of all, and then you would think I was rude."

The man held out a work-roughened hand. The calluses weren't thick or hard, like they'd surely been in his younger years, but his hand was still solid and thick.

"Good to meet you, Junior."

"Why are you taking cooking lessons?" Marshall asked while Smith shook Junior's hand.

Smith opened his mouth, but he hated to say that it was because he was trying to woo a woman. These men were probably taking cooking lessons just so they could feed themselves and survive life.

It seemed a little frivolous to be taking them just because he wanted to impress a girl. Frivolous and very junior high.

"It might make you more comfortable to find out that we're doing it to find women." Blaze nodded, giving Smith a slow wink as he did so.

"That's not entirely true. We don't want 'women,'" Junior said, emphasizing the men part of that, as in he didn't want a lot of women. "We just want one."

"I don't think we've decided on that specifically," Marshall disagreed.

"I don't really like the idea of sharing," Blaze said.

Smith swallowed. He thought maybe he had stepped into the wrong building. This wasn't the type of group that he wanted to be a part of.

"Would you guys stop it. You're making him uncomfortable." Jane, her voice holding teacher authority, reprimanded the men.

"What? We're being serious." Marshall looked affronted that she would step in and dress them down.

"You can tell him exactly what you're doing, because you know he's not getting the right impression right now," Jane said, with a hand on her hip, even though it held a spatula.

"All right. We're going to start a TikTok channel. It's called Three Old Coots and a Lady."

"TikTok?" Smith asked. That seemed like an app for the younger generation. He hadn't even gotten on TikTok. Although he was adept at texting.

"Yeah. It's the up-and-coming thing. Everyone's on it."

"I'm not," Smith said reasonably, since everyone meant everyone, and if one person wasn't, then not everyone was.

The men didn't seem interested in logic, though, because they were nodding their heads at Junior's statement.

"We're going to make a gazillion dollars because people are going to love our cooking videos. The only problem is, we don't cook."

"Also, we don't have a lady," Junior reminded them. "We kind of need one, since the channel is Three Old Coots and a Lady."

"Details. We'll worry about that when we can actually cook."

Smith bit his lips. Trying not to laugh at three old men who couldn't cook, starting a cooking channel, never mind the fact that they had a lady in the title and no lady to cook with them.

"You could hire someone." He tried to be helpful. After all, if this was the class he was going to be joining, he wanted to be able to fit in.

"We don't know if we can make any money. We can't pay her when none of us are making anything. That wouldn't be fair." Junior's answer was easily said, like they'd already discussed this.

"I suggested they just name their channel Three Old Coots, and if they happen to attract a lady, then they could add 'and a Lady' when they actually have one. But they're insisting that Three Old Coots doesn't have the same ring as Three Old Coots and a Lady,"

Jane said. Her smile was affectionate, like she loved the old men and thought they were adorable.

"So you know about this?" Smith asked, wondering why she wasn't the lady.

"We were talking about it at our table. We eat breakfast here every morning. After all, we don't cook, remember?" Marshall started out with the explanation.

"Miss Jane heard us talking about it, maybe not about the TikTok channel, but about us not being able to cook. After all, I can boil water and drop hot dogs into it. So, we have one meal. But that's just one video. Although, I think if I missed the pan the first time I dropped the hot dogs in, we could make it into two videos. You know, kind of like a 'to be continued' thing where people are on the edge of their seat wondering what happened and have to watch the sequel, you know? What is the old man going to do now that he dropped his hot dogs on the floor? Break to commercial, and the next day, you come back and you find out that I happen to have two packs of hot dogs in my refrigerator, so my dog eats the cold ones off the floor, and I cook the second pack in the water."

"I'm telling you, no one is going to watch that. We need to have a lady in it. People don't want to see an old coot dropping hot dogs on the floor." Blaze rolled his eyes.

"I would make it funny. Plus, they'd watch just so they could see my hair." Junior, the only one who actually still had more than five strands of hair, patted his head like it was a crown. Or some kind of major accomplishment to have made it to his age and somehow managed to keep from scaring all of his hair off of his head throughout his lifetime.

"Even if it's funny, you still need a lady." Marshall seemed stubbornly determined to not do a channel without a lady.

Smith cleared his throat. "Maybe there will be a lady who joins your group, one who needs to learn how to cook." He wondered if they were ever going to actually get to the cooking lesson. Although, talking to the old men was entertaining.

"We need a lady who knows how to cook. Not someone like us."

"So, you're looking for someone who's better than you, but you don't want to pay her?" Smith figured there was a lack of logic there somewhere, but he couldn't quite articulate what it was.

"We can't pay her if we're not making money. We already said that. Boy, I sure hope you never try to start your own business. You gotta make money." Blaze nodded his head as though to emphasize his point.

"Actually, I'm hoping to start ranching soon." It might not be ranching. He might end up working on a produce farm. Somehow, that didn't seem like such a bad thing. Not like it might have been a week ago when he thought about it. But it seemed to be something that Abrielle loved, and he could see himself getting involved in it too. Going to the farmers market had been fun.

"Ranching?" Junior asked. "I was a rancher. If you need some advice, I can give you some."

"His advice will be: don't do it," Marshall said.

"All right. I'm glad you guys got to know each other a little bit, but I think it's time to get started. I've been advertising our Crockpot Cream Cheese Chicken Chili for a week now, and people are going to be lining up at the door at six o'clock wanting it, and we need to have it ready."

"She has a lot of faith. She thinks our first lesson, the first day of class, we're actually going to make a meal the people are going to want to eat. I'm thinking not." Blaze shook his head sadly, as though already commiserating with Jane who was going to be most assuredly disappointed with the abilities of her class.

"Have faith, old man," Marshall said, patting his arm.

"Who are you calling old man? You're older than I am," Blaze said sourly.

"By three weeks. What's three weeks when you're our age?"

"Three weeks is three weeks. It means you're older than me."

"All right, so you have to start with a crockpot, of course. Do all of you have crockpots?"

The old man nodded, and Marshall said, "We went together, got the change out of our couch cushions and out of the bin where we'd been keeping it for years, rolled it up, and bought enough stuff to stock one kitchen between the three of us. I'm keeping this stuff because I have the best kitchen."

Smith couldn't help but be surprised. They were actually going to try to do this. They'd already taken steps to accomplish what they wanted.

"Do any of you have a way of recording it?" he asked, because in his experience, older folks typically didn't know how to run their smartphones, at least the video part of it.

He needn't have worried; all three of the men reached into their back pockets almost as one person and held up their phones.

"We've been practicing. Do you want to see some of our videos?" Junior asked, pulling his phone down and starting to swipe on it.

"Could we do that after class, please?" Jane asked, and Smith had to hand it to her. She didn't look frazzled at all. Well, not very frazzled. She did look at her watch twice, as though she were concerned about whether or not they were going to have this ready in time for people to eat at the diner.

"Yeah. Sorry," Junior mumbled, shoving his phone back in his pocket.

"So, I know the men have a crockpot at home. I also have four more crockpots here, so once I do this one, we have the ingredients to make four more. Hopefully we get the crowd I'm expecting later tonight." She did have a little bit of worry cross her features as she said that, and Smith made a note that he could take some home with him.

Or maybe he could get Abrielle to eat with him at the diner. Did a person ask the person they were considering having a marriage of convenience with out on a date?

Was eating at the diner a date?

Those were questions he didn't know the answers to.

"All right, Smith, I have one crockpot left for you." Jane gave an easy smile.

"I hope no one else comes in," Blaze muttered.

"We'll just have someone share a crockpot. It won't be a big deal," Jane said soothingly, although it didn't erase the wrinkle in Blaze's forehead.

"All right, you get two chicken breasts, and you put them in your crockpot first." Jane pointed to the pile of chicken breasts that she must have prepared earlier.

The men did it, in silence for the most part, because, as much goofing off as they had done, it was pretty obvious that they all truly wanted to learn how to cook. Smith found it hard to believe that they actually thought they were going to start a TikTok channel that was going to be successful, but he loved that they had the gumption to be doing something like that at their age. He thought it sounded a lot more fun than sitting around playing checkers, but maybe when he was that age, that's all he would want to do. He couldn't say.

"All right, now that you have that done, we're going to add corn, black beans, the diced tomatoes with green chilis, chicken broth, cumin, chili powder, onion powder, and the ranch seasoning. Oh, also the bacon, which I cooked and chopped earlier." Jane's smile was devious. "If I know men, it would be impossible for them to actually cook the bacon and have enough left to put in the crockpot for the recipe. When you do this at home, you can do it however you want to, but since I wanted bacon for our meal, I decided I'd better cook it myself."

"When we get our lady for the Three Old Coots channel, we need a wise one. Just like Jane."

Smith tried not to giggle at the seriousness of Junior's words. After all, Jane was absolutely correct. He'd never cooked bacon without eating at least half of it before he set it on the table.

There was a bunch of scrambling around as all the men tried to get the different things that Jane had set out for them, the chicken broth being the hardest since they had to measure two cups.

Junior had forgotten his glasses and couldn't read the measuring cup, and Smith ended up doing it for him. It was the first time in his life he managed to read a measuring cup, and he had to admit it wasn't as hard as he would have thought it would have been with all the lines and numbers and words on the side of it.

All that was left was simply putting the cream cheese on the top, covering it with the lid, and allowing it to cook for five hours.

"All right. I have recipe cards printed out for each of you, although, Smith, you'll have to use mine."

Smith took the card she offered. "I'm sorry. I didn't realize I was supposed to sign up."

"No. You weren't. But I originally scheduled the class just for Marshall, Blaze, and Junior. And I really didn't expect anyone else to stop in. I'm thrilled that you did, and if you're coming back, I'll make sure we have enough supplies for next time."

"I'm not sure if I'll be back. I suppose it depends on how this goes."

"What do you mean on how this goes?" Marshall asked as he looked at his own recipe card, squinting as though he'd never seen words in his life before. "Cooking is a lot easier when you have someone to show you what to do."

"That's the whole point of our TikTok channel," Junior said, as though that were obvious.

"I know. But I need someone to show me what to do so I can do the TikTok channel."

"Once you do it a few times, it'll get easier. The more you cook, the better you get at it. Just like anything else that you've done in your life." Jane's words were soothing, and some of the scowl left Marshall's face.

Chapter 19

"You didn't answer my question?" Marshall asked, looking at Smith.

Normally, Smith wouldn't talk about something like this to anyone, but maybe the old guys would actually have some advice for him. It might not be good advice, but sometimes bad advice could make a person see where they were going wrong

"I'm thinking about a marriage of convenience. I didn't make a very good impression on the girl who's thinking about marrying me, and I thought maybe if I could cook a meal for her, she would soften toward me a little."

"You mean she doesn't want to marry you at all?" Blaze asked, folding the card up carefully before he dug his bulging billfold out of his pocket and tucked it in, picking up several pieces of paper that fell out and sticking them back in as well.

"Well, I don't think we're getting married in the typical sense, you know, because we love each other and all that." Smith wondered why he thought this was a good idea. He had no easy way of saying this, and the men were all looking at him like he was nuts in the head, which was making him think that maybe he was.

"Go on," Marshall encouraged, holding his own card absentmindedly, as though he'd already forgotten about it.

"Basically, if we want to own a ranch, we have to get married."

"Oh. You must be Miss April's nephew. I hadn't put the two of you together yet." Marshall snapped his fingers.

"You must be talking about Abrielle. She's the one who's living on Miss April's ranch."

"Yeah." They obviously knew more than he did about the situation. Maybe they even knew more than he did about himself.

"Well, that little girl works pretty hard. I think making a meal for her would be a great idea." Blaze nodded his head. "Now, tell me more about this marriage of convenience thing." He looked around at his buddies. "Listen closely, boys. This might be the way we get our lady."

Smith hesitated. Did he really want to say this to the men and possibly subject some woman to a proposition of a marriage of convenience to one of them?

That was not giving the lady enough credit. If she wanted to say no, she could.

With that thought in mind, Smith said, "A marriage of convenience is where you decide to get married without dating, or loving each other, or maybe even knowing each other. You just know that you have character and integrity, and the other person does too, and you're willing to make promises that you're going to keep for the rest of your life."

That seemed like such a long time. Did he really want to make promises to someone else that he was going to have to keep for the rest of his life?

It seemed like such a big step.

But he wanted the ranch.

"I guess, if you want something bad enough, you have to make a trade-off. And I want the ranch, and in return, I have to marry Abrielle."

"I know you're not asking me, but can I just say, that is the absolute worst thing you could ever say, and if Abrielle heard that, it would definitely hurt her feelings, marriage of convenience or no." Jane spoke from the sink where she was washing the cutting board where the chicken had been sitting, and she looked up at him, biting her lip with her brows drawn down, worry stamped on her face.

"We're not deluding each other that we have feelings for each other."

"But if you're going to spend the rest of your lives living together, there's going to have to be some kind of feeling there. I know Abrielle is a strong woman, but no one wants to live with a man who is just with her because of what she has. She wants to know that if he isn't madly 'in love' with her," she used air quotes when she said in love, "that he admires and respects her. If it's because of her character and integrity, so be it. But that she has something in her person that draws you. Not just her property."

Jane looked at him for another second or two before she turned back to the dishwater.

Smith was quiet, thinking about it. Realizing she was probably right. He didn't really want to go that route, although he already admitted to himself that there was something about Abrielle that was different than the other women he knew. But he had already been down that road and knew women, at least the women he knew, weren't anything he wanted to trust with any of his tender feelings. He didn't even want to admit he had tender feelings when he was around women.

"So you're saying we couldn't get her to marry one of us, just so she could be part of our TikTok channel? It could make a lot of money. Surely that would be a draw?" Junior scratched his head and then smoothed his hair back down, patting it with what Smith would term a little extra love.

"You can't make it about the money," Jane said, without turning around. "At least, not to the kind of girl that you want to be with. To be married to."

She didn't look at them, and that said to Smith that maybe she was a little bit more upset about it than what she wanted to let on.

She was probably right. There were good women in the world. He just had a bad experience.

"If you had something in your past that makes you not trust women, maybe you should talk to Abrielle about it. I can tell you, just from the short time I've been here, and how well everyone in town talks about her, that she's not the kind of woman who's going to marry someone for their ranch, use them, and take what she can from them before she discards them."

Again, Jane didn't turn around, and Smith wondered how she had any clue of what was going on in his mind. Maybe his attitude was more prevalent than what he thought.

Or maybe, it wasn't a woman thing, but it was a human thing.

He wasn't sure where that came from, but it seemed like a good thought.

"I don't think she's interested in hearing my past," he mumbled as he walked over to the sink to wash his hands.

"I think you'd be surprised. Sometimes when we explain our past, it makes our actions of the present and future make more sense. People can understand why we are the way we are, and sometimes they can even help us grow out of it, but no matter what kind of experience you had, you have to allow it to make you better, not bitter."

"She's right." Marshall fingered the card still in his hand. "A lot of bad things are going to happen in your life. A lot of times, you're going to meet people who aren't kind and who treat you a lot worse than what anyone should ever be treated. You have to allow those people to teach you things, to help you grow, but not to stunt your growth, that's what being bitter is. It stunts your growth."

"Then you end up becoming just like them. Or else so closed off and cold that you're not a help to mankind. You're just a drag." Junior sounded like he knew what he was talking about.

"No one here is saying it's easy. But we've all been through it. Had people double-cross us in business, or relationships, and even our kids. Sometimes it's the people who are closest to you that hurt the worst." Blaze shrugged a broad, bony shoulder, like there wasn't anything he could do about it.

All the men nodded sagely.

"You have to learn to let the hurt roll off of you while you forgive and continue to be kind," Jane agreed, rinsing the cutting board off and setting it long end up on the counter.

"She's right. We wouldn't be thinking about starting a TikTok channel, trusting each other to go into it, and even bringing someone else on board, a woman no less, if we hadn't let the things that happened in our past go. That's the key to having an old age that is joyful and productive." Marshall seemed to feel passionate about that subject.

Was that really the key?

"Just so you're aware, no one's expecting you to do that by yourself. You have to talk to Jesus about it. Because things that are impossible for man to do on his own are possible through God. And I'm not just saying that as lip service. I'm saying that as someone who's lived it." Marshall looked as serious as he had looked the entire time, and Smith had no doubt he was speaking from experience.

He had faith, but was his faith that strong? Strong enough for him to trust God to allow him to forgive, to learn, and to get better?

He wasn't sure. It felt like it would be a lot easier to just cut people out of his life and move on.

"I don't think anyone here is saying that you have to stay with someone who treats you badly, although I've seen it done, and it is possible. Even to live a joyful life in that kind of situation. But that takes a true dependence on Jesus. And not many people can do it."

"I don't think I have to worry about any of that with Abrielle. She's not a mean or vindictive person." He'd experienced that firsthand Saturday morning when she returned his unkindness of the previous night with grace. He hadn't even been able to get her upset. She had been determined that no matter what he did, she wasn't going to get upset.

Wasn't that what the men were telling him he needed to do? That no matter what people did to him, he could not allow it to affect him.

"I can't say for sure that I'm going to be back next week, but I appreciate the instruction this week. Are you sure I don't owe you anything?" He looked around at the men, but he directed his question to Jane.

"You don't owe me anything. You helped me make supper for my patrons tonight. I should be paying you, but since that wasn't part of the agreement..." She grinned, the seriousness sliding off her face and the joy coming back.

He jerked his head. "Good to meet all of you. I'm sure I'll be seeing you all around."

They murmured a few words, and Smith walked out, thinking that maybe he was one step closer to making a decision.

The sound of pounding hooves said he was one step closer to being gored by that crazy cow again. He jerked back, more out of instinct than reflex, as Abrielle's crazy, man-eating cow and those vicious, long horns went flying by.

He glanced after the cow, not surprised to see the hog running across the road and disappearing between the barber shop and the bakery.

Also unsurprising was hearing fast footsteps and turning his head back to see Abrielle, her face set, her arms pumping, chugging after the cow as fast as she could go.

It was long gone by the time she reached him, but she wasn't slowing down, so he waited until she was five feet from him before he took a step out and stood in the middle of the sidewalk.

She screeched to a halt, a glare on her face, hands on her hips.

"I think we've been in his position before," he murmured casually, not nearly as upset the second time as he had been the first. In fact, he had to fight off the thought that Abrielle was...cute.

"I thought you learned your lesson the first time." Her words weren't short and there almost seemed to be a small smile floating around her lips.

He pointed to his shirt. "No new hole. So I guess I learned something. Not sure about you."

She pursed her lips and looked a little abashed. "I'm fighting the urge to say that you might be making sense."

"Don't fight the truth."

She smirked, but they didn't say anything more because Deuce and Teagan came strolling down the sidewalk.

"Anyone see a runaway pig?" Teagan asked.

Smith bit his lip, while Abrielle answered her. They started talking about the hog and how hard it was to catch and whose it might have been. Smith listened with one ear.

Deuce must have been doing the same because after about five minutes of the girls talking, he said, low to Smith, "That your pickup?"

Smith looked to where he nodded at the only pickup parked on the street.

"Yep."

"Nice toolbox." Deuce whistled low. "Custom made?"

"Yeah, a buddy of mine from the Airforce, a welder, put that together for me. Just something he did in his spare time."

"It's sweet. I've looked for something like that, and it makes sense that it's custom."

"Yeah. Hard to find something with those doors on the front."

"Extra storage."

"And easier to get to."

"If you ever want to sell it, let me know."

Smith shrugged. He wasn't attached to the toolbox, but definitely couldn't afford to replace it. "I will," he promised, but figuring he never would.

"You're not even listening!" Teagan said, her hands on her hips and her words directed to Deuce.

"I was talking trucks. I don't want to talk about that pig unless the word bacon's involved."

"I can't even believe you said that!" Teagan said, as she gave Abrielle a wave and took Deuce's arm, pulling him down the sidewalk in the direction the animals took.

"Why not? Ham, spare ribs, sausage..." His voice faded off before Teagan's fake-outraged sputters.

Smith smiled. Those two were a pair.

His eyes landed back on Abrielle. Would he ever have that type of easy relationship with someone he loved?

Chapter 20

"This is really good," Abrielle said as she swallowed another bite of chili that Smith had brought home with him.

"I agree. I hadn't expected it to taste this good."

Abrielle smiled at the surprise in his voice as he dug his spoon into the bowl and put another big spoonful in his mouth. "Why does that surprise you? Don't you cook?"

"This is the first meal I've ever made in my life before. Unless of course you count something I dumped from a can into a pan or made from a box. I don't even do the box stuff very well. I made about five boxes of macaroni and cheese that were really gluey before I realized I had to boil the water first."

She grimaced, tilting her head to look at him. "Why did you decide today, of all days, that you were going to learn to cook?"

When he had left earlier, he had just said there was a thing he wanted to go to, to give her privacy to visit with her friend.

That had been fine with her, since she hadn't minded having a little bit of time away from the constant of having to introduce him to everyone and explain why she was with him.

It hadn't occurred to her that he was going to a cooking class, although she heard bits and pieces about it at church, of course. She just hadn't put the two together.

Her question seemed to make him uneasy as he looked down at his bowl, his spoon pausing in midair, his shoulders flexing.

Finally, he didn't move anything but his head as he looked up.

The light in the kitchen blinked down, and all the appliances in the room that had become so familiar to her over the last two years seemed to hold their breath in anticipation as he paused before he spoke.

"I felt bad for what I did. I thought to myself, how can I help you? How can I make it up to you? And when I found out you were going to a friend's and there was a cooking class I could take at the same time, I thought it might be a way that I could...ease your burden a little. Just something I could do to make your life easier."

Her mouth hung open as she stared at him, her eyes running over his face, his body language, his sincere words.

Somewhere in the back of her mind, she remembered that her grandparents had told her that true love was looking at someone else and doing everything you could to make their life better. Easier. Giving yourself for them.

It went against a person's naturally selfish nature to give up what they wanted for themselves—their leisure time, their hobbies, things they enjoyed—and live to please someone else. Of course, in a perfect marriage, both partners would give and both would therefore receive.

Looking at Smith, with his manly man stride, his handsomeness, his confidence, she could hardly imagine that cooking was something that interested him or something he wanted to spend an afternoon learning to do.

But he'd done it for her.

Maybe she was more touched than what she should be, but she found her throat tightening and an odd sensation curling in her stomach. "You did that just for me?"

"I know. Sappy, isn't it? I'm sorry. I feel pathetic."

She blinked, her brows lowering before she shook her head and reached across the table, putting her hand over top of his where it lay beside his bowl. "It's not pathetic. It's...beautiful."

Maybe she shouldn't admit that. She wasn't entirely sure she could trust him, and that seemed like something he could throw back up in her face with the intention of hurting her, but it was the truth. "I can't believe you did that just for me. Spent an afternoon learning how to cook something and even bringing it home. That's...not something I've ever heard of anyone doing before."

In a normal relationship, using the word "normal" loosely, where people dated, the idea of buying a woman's meal was the sacrifice that a man was supposed to make. But that was just money. It didn't require actual time and brainpower, and while she supposed he was getting something out of it—the ability to cook—that might not be considered something that he appreciated, since he had never made the effort to learn before.

"Maybe I'm putting more weight to this decision than it deserves, but I'm touched. Thank you."

"It's the very least I could do after the way I treated you. I wasn't nice, and we both know it."

"You apologized. I forgave you. We...maybe didn't laugh about it, but I think we will someday, if we're still together."

"I have no intention of going into a marriage and not sticking it out."

"Me either. But sometimes our intentions don't always work out the way we want them to. And the things we think we will never do, we end up doing." She gave a shrug of her shoulders. "I never thought I'd be here on a farm in North Dakota growing produce, but I love it."

"Yeah. I guess you're right. This wasn't exactly the first plan that I had for my life either, but the farmers market was fun, and I'd like to learn more about growing produce."

"I'll teach you everything I know, and there's lots more for both of us to learn. I could only get into it as big as one person can do. With two people, we can do so much more if that's seriously something you're interested in?"

"Well, you've already started it, and while that wasn't what I had planned for the ranch—I was thinking cattle and crops—it seems like since you've already put the work in, it would be kind of rude of me to try to start my own thing."

"We don't have a mortgage payment. As long as we don't, the produce should more than support us. And it's something that could grow into something bigger." She knew she was getting excited about it. It was something she could talk on and on about and bore everyone around her. So she tried to contain herself. She didn't want to become that person who, every time she opened her mouth and looked like she was going to say the word produce, people scattered like rats in daylight.

"We shouldn't have a mortgage payment, so we can focus on growing the business."

She could be wrong, but he sounded kind of excited about it.

After Cassie had told her that she thought Smith could be the best decision of her life, it had really gotten Abrielle thinking.

She admired Cassie. After what she'd been through with the cancer, she had a tendency to do a lot of thinking and to have wisdom that someone who hadn't gone through something like that wouldn't have.

Abrielle highly valued her opinion, and the fact that she had given her stamp of approval meant a lot.

She knew Cassie wouldn't do that superficially.

Of course, the decision was ultimately hers, and she'd already decided she wanted to do what the Lord wanted her to do.

God gave a person godly friends for that exact reason—to help them see and make wise choices.

Her phone buzzed in her pocket.

She pulled it out. She had been living alone so long she forgot that it might be rude to look at her phone while they were eating.

"Do you mind?" she asked, having glimpsed the text and saw it was a number from Fargo. "I promise I won't make it a habit to spend dinner on my phone while I eat."

His lips curved a little, but he shrugged his shoulders. "Go ahead."

She gave him a tentative smile before she looked back down.

> This is Fresh Groceries in Fargo. We had spoken with you earlier this season about the possibility of you delivering bulk lettuce to our distribution center to be sold as lo-cally grown produce. At the time, we had a supplier lined up. They had issues on their farm and cannot fulfill their contract. We were wondering if it would be possible for you to deliver a truckload of lettuce to our store by 6 AM tomorrow morning?

She gasped, her hand going to her chest as she read the text again.

"What is it? Is everything okay?" Smith had put his spoon down and had pushed his chair back some, almost like he was getting ready to get up to go help her with whatever she needed.

Almost subconsciously, she realized that and appreciated it.

He would help her, without her even having to ask.

She put a hand up, and he visibly relaxed.

"This is a distributor I had contacted earlier this spring. One of the many." She glanced up and gave him a look that probably did nothing to convey the number of people that she contacted, trying to get a foot in the door with the lettuce that she had planted. "I grew way more lettuce than what I knew I could sell at the farmers markets. And I was hoping I could deliver some bulk lettuce to stores. No one had taken me up on my offer, until just now."

"They want your lettuce?" Smith asked, and there was excitement in his voice. Whether it was fabricated or real, she appreciated his support.

"They do." She knew her eyes were shining as she looked up at him, then her shoulders slumped. "But they want it tomorrow morning. There is no way I can pick the amount of lettuce that they want, tie it, box it, and have it in Fargo by six AM tomorrow." She looked at the time on her phone. "It's seven o'clock in the evening now. There's no way."

"What if I help you?"

She froze. It hadn't even occurred to her to ask him. Not because she didn't think he would help, just because she'd been alone so long, doing everything herself, she hadn't thought of asking him.

She ran over what she needed to do in her head. From picking the lettuce, wrapping, boxing it up...

"I have enough boxes in the shed. I have enough bands as well." She spoke thoughtfully. "If I were doing it myself, I would give myself an entire day, maybe a day and a half to pick and pack it, and then deliver it that night or early the next morning. With two of us, we could cut it down to six hours, maybe catch an hour or two of sleep, before we have to leave to be in Fargo."

"Or we could take it directly to Fargo and sleep in the parking lot until they're ready to unload?"

She grinned; that would have been her preference too. But she didn't want to make him think that she was going to make him work all night, with no rest.

"I like that idea," she said simply.

He grinned. Then he sobered. "Are you sure you have enough lettuce?"

"I haven't had a chance to show you around the farm. I put up a low rowhouse last fall, and I planted it full of lettuce, thinking that I had enough leads that I would get a buyer. Of course I didn't, and so all of my lettuce, which is at peak freshness right now, was going to go to waste. This is about the best thing that could have happened."

"It must be a God thing," he said simply.

She loved that he thought that way. That thought had been in her mind too, but the fact that he didn't want to blame it on luck, but that he could see the hand of his Creator guiding their lives, made her feel secure in a way that nothing else could have.

It also gave him one more point in his favor, and she considered whether or not a marriage of convenience was a good idea.

"I think it is."

She couldn't help but wonder if maybe it was a good thing of course. It would help her with her produce business. But maybe it was also God showing her that when something happened, Smith was going to jump to her side to help. And it would give her a chance to see how they worked together. And for him to see, too. Because the decision wasn't just hers. He had to decide that she was someone he could live with as well.

"All right. Let's finish eating, and then we can make a plan to get started."

"Sounds good. I'll clear off the table and take care of the dishes. Also I'll put the leftovers away, and we should have enough to give us a little breakfast before we head to Fargo."

"I really like this cooking class. Not only was the meal delicious, but it came at a perfect time."

"Funny how the Lord worked things out that way."

They smiled together and finished eating.

When they were done, true to his word, he took care of the dishes while she grabbed a flashlight and went outside.

The first thing she needed to do was get the boxes, at least enough to get started. She had been in the shed two days prior to get the boxes she needed to take to the farmers market, so she knew there were plenty of boxes in it.

Sure enough, when she opened it up, they were there right where she had left them.

Some were already put together, and some were just in flat stacks that would need to be shaped into box form.

Grabbing the ones that were already put together, she also found the bag of ties and her knife and walked to the low rowhouse.

"You want me over there?" Smith called from the porch, and she heard his boots come down the steps.

"Please."

He definitely hurried through the dishes, and she smiled to herself, appreciating the fact that he was hurrying for her.

"I wish I had a light or something that we could work by. I've never done this in the dark," she said as he reached her side, and she led the way to the low rowhouse.

"I might be able to rig something up. I'd need about twenty minutes and your flashlight, but if that makes our work go faster, it might be worth it."

"I think it would." She hadn't even considered rigging a light up. That was a great idea.

"Let me see the flashlight," he said, holding out his hand.

She put it in his hand without questioning him.

He shone it around, looked at the ceiling for a bit, and seemed to be thinking. "Do you have any rope?"

"In the shed. I'll go back, and we can both carry some more boxes over. We'll need them eventually."

He walked beside her over to the shed where she grabbed some rope.

On the way back, she explained to him what they were going to do with the lettuce so when they got back to the low rowhouse, she was able to show him, reiterating what she had already said.

It wasn't difficult, and he caught on quickly. Once he'd done it several times, she continued to work while he took the flashlight, found an angle that would work where the lettuce wouldn't be in shadow for either one of them, and strung it up.

She had to admit the idea was brilliant, and she appreciated him thinking about it.

Within twenty minutes, they were working silently, side by side, quickly but carefully packing the lettuce.

"I'm glad it's not that cold out."

"'Not that cold' is relative. I've been in North Carolina for a few years, and this is pretty chilly for me."

"It's above freezing, and that's kind of my litmus test. Anything above freezing is not that cold."

He laughed at the humor in her voice, and she realized that to someone from North Carolina, not that cold really was relative.

"Does it even get below freezing in North Carolina?"

"Oh sure. In the winter. But this time of year, it feels more like summer and things have been growing for a while. There is a definite lag when you come up here. This feels like about February to me."

"I can't imagine living in a warmer climate. But I suppose that would be nice. Being outside from February on."

"It is nice, but it gets really hot in the summer. You almost have to be back inside, in order to survive. Unless you can really take the heat."

Chapter 21

"So, what made you leave North Carolina?" Abrielle snapped a band on a bunch of lettuce and put it in the box they had set between them. "If I'm not prying."

"You're not prying. I suppose, if we go through with this marriage, you should know anyway."

"That's kind of what I was thinking, but some people get annoyed when you dig into their background. They don't want to dredge up old memories or something, I guess."

"Or make themselves look bad. Which is kind of why I would drag my feet."

"That bad?"

"I don't know. I feel like it wasn't my fault." He sighed.

She definitely got the impression he really didn't want to talk about it. But that it was something he was doing for her. She liked the fact that he would do things that he didn't particularly want to, just for her. It made her wonder, though, if it was something that he would continue after they were married. Or was this just something he was doing to get her to agree to be with him?

He didn't seem like that kind of man. The kind of man who put on a show with things he didn't mean.

"After I got out of the Air Force, it's kind of a hard adjustment, getting back to civilian life. I mean, you feel free, like a burden's been lifted in one way, but it's also something where you feel like you don't really fit in anymore. You've experienced things that no one else around you has. You know things that no one else knows. You know how to kill people."

"Ouch. I never thought of it like that. That's tough."

"Yeah. But that's the military. That's what you're there for."

"To learn how to kill people."

"To defend your country, which is probably about the same thing. Although, it's less about hand-to-hand combat and more about missile strikes and using a new type of warfare. I was ground support anyway. But there are still guns involved."

"Of course."

"Anyway. I worked in a company, doing repair work, so the same things I'd done in the Air Force, just a little different. And I got in with the owner's daughter. I wasn't with her because of her dad, but I guess it could look that way. Anyway, we decided to start our own business. Her dad was retiring, and she wanted to take it over. I had a nest egg, what I had saved from being in the military—it doesn't pay that well, but you really don't need to spend money. Not if you choose not to. And I was looking for a place to invest it in. Investing in our own business sounded like a really good idea."

"I agree. There's just something about owning your own business, having the authority to decide what you want to do, that really makes sense."

"Yeah. Sounds good anyway. She was the resident authority, because she'd been in business for a long time. But she promised that I would be half owner and that I would have just as much say as she would. And it seemed silly for me to insist on getting everything in writing. Especially given our relationship."

"You were afraid of offending her by asking for that, but you didn't trust her?"

"Exactly. Stupid on my part now, looking back. But I guess it was a decision I made with my emotions."

"Or it was a decision you made with the wrong person."

He didn't say anything for a little while, and she wondered if she pushed too far. She hadn't meant to imply that she was the right person with that comment, but it kind of came off that way. And she could have meant it that way. After all, she had every intention of keeping her word.

"Yeah. I guess that's exactly right. I had other girlfriends in the military and even before that, and I guess with Kylie, that was her name, by the way, I hadn't quite gotten to the point where I thought that all women were just out to get what they could from a man, but Kylie kind of sealed the deal. She ended up taking everything when she broke up with me. And while I have text messages and emails of things that we said back and forth and there were a few things we signed, although I didn't get a copy, and I don't have any contracts in writing. Nothing to say that the money I gave her was not hers but ours."

"And so you never got your money back?"

"No. I'd have to hire a lawyer, and she has far more money than I do to do that and to fight me. I did talk to a friend of mine who is an attorney, and he was going to do a little digging for free, on the side, but I'm really not interested, as much as I'd like my money back. I suppose, at least I would hope, that I would win a court fight, eventually, since I'm right. But I just didn't think it was worth it. I thought it was better to cut my losses and leave. Especially when Aunt April said there was a ranch in North Dakota that I could have."

She swallowed hard, her fingers cold, but she hardly noticed. After all, it made her feel guilty, this man who had been hoping that the ranch that she was on right now was his salvation, and finding out that it came with her, too.

"I'm sorry." Her voice was small, and it barely made any sound as it settled between them.

"Sorry about what? About Kylie? There's nothing you could have done. I was the one who was stupid."

"I don't think trusting people is stupid. I think, I think when you trust people and they stab you in the back, they're the ones who are stupid. Because God is bigger than all that. We like to think He doesn't see that, or He doesn't meddle in the affairs of men, and sometimes He doesn't. But He is the righteous judge, and I'm sure that He's keeping track. He'll make sure that people get what's coming to them, whether it's here, or whether it's at the Great Throne Judgment."

"I'm glad you're confident of that. Looks to me, last time I checked anyway, that Kylie was doing pretty good for herself, and God hadn't intervened at all."

"If she's not saved, she'll have eternity in hell to think about all the ways she could have been better to people. She doesn't need to suffer in this life."

She wasn't sure whether he agreed with her or not. He didn't say anything for a long time.

They filled up the next box and set it aside and started on another one.

Finally his voice broke the companionable silence that had descended. "I had never considered it that way. I suppose I want to see them get their just desserts here. I want to see people who aren't honest be punished for it right away. I don't want to wait on God to maybe or maybe not make sure they get what's coming to them. I want to know life is fair."

"I think that's natural. I think that's what we all want. But God has a bigger picture. He sees more than what we do."

"So you've never been around someone who stabbed you in the back?"

"I worked in the corporate world. I was around people like that all the time. That's part of the reason I'm so happy here on the farm. It was nice to get out of the rat race, to get away from the people who were only after what they could get for themselves. Of course there were the ones who did the least amount possible, who did their job but absolutely no more and had no interest in helping anyone. The people who couldn't see anyone but themselves."

"Uninterested in anything having to do with their job?"

"Yeah. And just general disregard for anyone around them. You know, nice when they had to be, but nothing more. It's so much different in Sweet Water. Everyone is concerned about everyone else. I mean, of course there are people who don't get along with each other."

"Are there? I haven't met any like that?"

"Well, you met Deuce. One of his buddies, Cormac, absolutely cannot stand one of Deuce's sisters. It's like the big quarrel in town. Everyone always enjoys trying to put them together anytime they can. You know like if there's a live nativity, someone will ask Brooklyn to be Mary, and someone else will ask Cormac to be Joseph. Maybe the town isn't as nice as what I like to think it is, because everyone takes perverse pleasure anytime they're able to pull one of those things off."

"Wow. That's sadistic."

"It sure is. I think the last time they did it, they had them working a booth together at the fall festival. Bottle rings or something. They managed to do it for an entire day without saying one word to each other. I don't even know how that's possible, but they pulled it off."

"What happened to make them hate each other so much?"

"I'm not sure. Something back in high school. That's what I've heard. But that's one of the things about small towns, everyone knows, and for me to ask feels like prying."

"I see. Maybe I can nose around some. Although, I guess it doesn't matter."

"Yeah, I know it doesn't matter, but I'm so curious."

He laughed, and maybe she shouldn't have admitted it. It was kind of like digging for gossip. Only she wasn't digging. She hadn't asked. She just wondered.

"You worked in the corporate world. Why did you come to Sweet Water?"

"I got fired."

"You got fired?"

"Well, laid off. I guess it's the same thing, because I didn't have any severance pay or anything. They just cut us."

"Ouch."

"I know. And that was about the time that my fiancé broke up with me."

"I forgot. You were engaged?"

Her stomach dropped. She'd meant to tell him about her engagement, but it had slipped her mind.

She balled her fingers up in fists and shoved them underneath her armpits to warm them up. After a few seconds, she pulled them back out and got to work again.

"Yeah. I'm sorry. I know that is something that I needed to talk to you about, but... It hasn't been that long. Even though it feels like we've been together and have been talking about a marriage of convenience for a really long time."

"A lot has happened today. And this whole lettuce thing is making it all take even longer."

"Yeah. Anytime you're up all night feels like forever."

"You've done this before?"

"Not much. Part of the reason that I'm here in Sweet Water and I settled on the ranch is because I wanted a slower life. I didn't always want to be pushed to do everything I had to do. Does that make sense?"

"Yeah. I get that. And that would defeat the point if you stayed up working your fingers to the bone."

"Exactly. What's the point of coming here, to relax and enjoy a slower life, if I pull all-nighters all the time?"

"I get it. But this was too good of an opportunity to pass up, I assume."

"Yeah. Although, if it hadn't been for you, I probably would have passed on it, just because I know I couldn't have done it by myself."

"So two are better than one?"

"I think that's true for almost anything, isn't it?"

He didn't answer her question, and they lapsed into silence for a bit. She had been thinking that she would walk through life alone, but so much of life was better if it was shared.

Of course, that meant giving up one's way and maybe compromising on other things. There were some things it was nice to just do and have alone. Things you didn't have to share if you weren't married.

But that meant not having a life partner, and while the trade-off sometimes seemed worth it, the last two years of being alone had told her that maybe it wasn't.

"Are you going to tell me about your fiancé?"

"He cheated." Surprised that she was able to say that without the pain that had pierced her heart for so long, she actually smiled. "It feels good to be able to say that and not hurt over it."

"A jerk. And it wasn't long ago?"

His question sounded casual, but she detected a bit of tension under his easy words.

"Yeah. Right around the time I lost my job. It's funny how sometimes in life everything seems to happen all at once."

"That's the truth. That whole when it rains, it pours thing."

"Yeah. That's exactly what I was thinking." She thought about what she wanted to say and then began, "I had planned the wedding. He wasn't super interested in anything, and I guess I should have taken that as a sign. But I just figured he didn't like big celebrations and I did, so I was the one who should be putting everything together. It ended up that when I had to cancel everything, I was the one who was out all the money. Which I suppose was nice for him."

"You don't say. I guess if you're with someone who allows you to do all the work while they do nothing, even if they're not interested, that should be a red flag."

She thought about him, out here putting lettuce together, when surely he had better things to do, things he was more interested in. While she was pretty sure he wasn't talking about himself, it definitely applied. "I guess he never actually admitted he cheated. I just had several people tell me he did, and maybe not surprisingly, when I broke up with him, he didn't admit it, but he was out with someone else the next night."

"I see."

"So, he could have cheated on the person he was cheating with?" She laughed, and he seemed startled before he joined her.

"A few hours is really fast to find a new girlfriend."

"Yeah. But I guess I don't have a whole lot to say, not if I meet you one week and marry you the next."

"I'd have to say you win. If it was a competition anyway."

"I am definitely not in competition with him. I haven't actually seen him since I moved here. And don't really care to." She paused for a second, thinking about it hard before she said, "I don't think I hate him. I might have at one time. I definitely hated the idea that anything good would happen to him, but I guess I'm over that now."

"They say time heals everything. I'm not really at the point where... I don't want to be bitter against Kylie. But I still resent the fact that I lost all my money. I know it was my fault. My stupidity. And... I guess that's my biggest thing with this whole marriage of convenience. I don't want to lose everything again."

"I guess we could have a prenup. Saying that if anything happens, we split the farm." She hated that, though. The idea that they were planning on splitting before they even got married. It just... A prenup just screamed their marriage wasn't going to last.

"No. I know that if I learned my lesson the way some people think I should have learned it, that solution would be the exact solution I would push for. But... Maybe I have just enough perspective now, and have just enough wisdom in my life, to realize that while I don't hate contracts and would sign one if I needed to, I don't think I want to have to live my life that way. I want to be able to trust people. Maybe that's crazy, but I'll depend on God to keep things straight."

"That's more faith than most people have. I'm not sure I have that much. Although," she added hastily, "I don't want a prenup. Just because..."

"It says we don't have faith in what we're doing?"

"Exactly. It's probably a wise move for some people, but not a move that goes along with my values and morals."

She couldn't believe he was agreeing with her. Especially after what happened to him with his girlfriend and losing his money. She couldn't believe he wasn't demanding a prenup.

"I was pretty bitter against women for a long time. I blamed the entire female gender for what happened. And even when Aunt April suggested we get married... I guess that was part of what I was doing on Friday, trying to get you to hate me. Because you're a woman, and I didn't trust you. I certainly didn't want to get married to you."

"Thanks." She said it lightly, sarcastically, and he smiled.

"But the way you reacted to me. The way you didn't allow me to make you angry. The way you decided to divide the kitchen in half, even." They laughed over that. "And then you admitted that you were being ridiculous. It all kind of worked together to show me that you weren't the same. It wasn't fair of me to lump you in with people like Kylie. Even when I first knew her, she wasn't the kind of person who was going to overlook something that someone else had done to her. She was going to demand retribution, if not an abject and groveling apology."

"That's probably what society would say that I deserved. But I don't think we should necessarily live demanding to get what we 'deserve.'"

"I agree. And I could see that in you. Which was what changed my mind."

By that time, they had filled enough boxes that Abrielle said, "As soon as we finish filling this one, I'll grab the box truck and bring it over. We'll put the boxes on the back. And stack them in the best we can. People who do this all the time have better systems, but I needed one that would work for farmers markets more than for bulk selling."

"Makes sense. You show me what to do, and I'll help you." He moved forward a little and then said, "There are a few places where the support is not as good as it should be, and a couple places where it looks like boards have fallen down. Is it okay if I work on that if I get any spare time?"

"I would love it!" she said immediately. "I can get plants to grow, but building something like this was a real stretch of my abilities. Keeping up with maintenance is definitely not something I'm good at."

"It's actually one of the things I *am* good at. I don't know anything about growing stuff. Kind of funny now that I was thinking about growing crops and ranching, when I know nothing about it. I suppose we always have inflated ideas of our own knowledge and abilities until we actually try to do something."

"The human condition, I suppose."

They laughed together, and it shocked her that they were kind of talking like old friends. She felt like she'd known him a lot longer than the amount of time they'd been together.

He was just easy to talk to and seemed thoughtful and considerate as well.

As the night progressed and the truck got fuller, they lapsed into silence more and more often, but the silences were easy, companionable, and not awkward.

By two AM, the truck was full and they were both dragging.

"I thought it would be a good idea to take the truck in immediately and sleep there. But..." She yawned as he pulled the back of the truck down and locked it. "I think I might need a nap before I drive in."

"I'd offer to drive, but I think I need the same thing. A nap."

Chapter 22

They walked to the house, side by side, and Abrielle felt like she had someone in her corner for the first time in a long time.

When they reached the door, Smith opened it for her, and she murmured a thank you.

"I'm going to change my clothes, and then I'm going to come down to the couch and lie down. If I go to my bed, I might end up sleeping way longer than what I want to."

"All right. I'll do the same."

She hadn't meant to make him feel like he needed to, but she appreciated that he was throwing himself into the farmwork and didn't want to discourage him. Or make him feel like she didn't appreciate it.

He allowed her to go up the stairs first, and he was waiting for her in the hall by the time she changed her clothes with his already changed.

He allowed her to go down the steps in front of him and followed her down.

They walked into the living room together, and she said, "Do you mind setting the alarm on your phone? And I'll set my alarm, and surely between the two of us, we can get up."

"That's fine. Just tell me what time."

They sorted out the time and set their phones down on the coffee table. He sat down on one end of the couch, and she sat down on the other.

"You really don't have to stay with me. This is going far above and beyond anything anyone expects you to do." She felt compelled to say that, even though he hadn't been acting like it was a hard thing or an imposition at all.

"I know. I want to. If this is going to be something that we're doing together, then we're doing it together. It's not going to be me doing all the easy stuff while you pull the all-nighters and go out of your way to make things work. It's going to be both of us working."

His tone was firm, and she didn't argue.

She managed not to sigh as she leaned back, putting her head down on the back of the couch. "I've wanted to do this since about nine o'clock this evening."

"Yeah. Me too. Bending over like that really makes my back hurt."

"That's pretty much a part of produce farming. Your back hurts, daily."

"Thanks for the warning. I guess I'll have to take that into consideration with everything else."

She closed her eyes, but his words penetrated, and she said, "So you're considering this? Running things over in your head? Trying to decide if this is something God wants us to do, or if this is just...something we want to do in order to have the farm?"

"Yeah. Pretty much all of that."

His voice was subdued, like he was drifting off to sleep already, while she always had a little bit of a hard time trying to shut her brain down. Make it relax so she could sleep. Convince it that tomorrow it could start thinking again just as soon as she opened her eyes. It never wanted to stop.

Sure enough, she barely breathed three more times and she heard light snoring coming from the other side of the couch.

The temperature had dropped, and she wished she'd turned the heat up in the house just a little bit or grabbed a blanket. But she didn't want to get snugly warm. She was usually a light sleeper and figured she'd definitely wake up to two alarms, but this was important enough that she didn't want to risk it.

If she thought she could make it, she would have driven down before she slept, but she didn't want to fall asleep while driving and never make it or, worse yet, hurt someone in the process.

She wasn't quite sure when her brain shut off and she drifted into sleep, but she awoke with a start.

At least her eyes flew open, and she wondered where she was, what was going on, and where all that noise was coming from.

It took her several seconds before she remembered about the phones and the alarms and the lettuce and the fact that she had a loaded truck that needed to go to Fargo.

Then she remembered about the man.

Mostly because somehow she had gone from sitting on her side of the couch to lying with her head kind of on his stomach and his torso leaning behind her, with his arm over her stomach and his head resting on it.

They'd somehow gotten twisted together, and while it was a little bit funny, it was also scary.

Maybe it was because she was just waking up, or maybe it was because she hadn't considered the whole being married for real thing, but the idea of a marriage of convenience was different than the idea of a real marriage.

One where it would be normal to sleep beside a man and wake up next to him.

She had been so focused on making promises she wasn't sure she could keep. Lifetime promises. She hadn't considered what actually went on in a marriage.

The alarms went on for several more seconds, and as she moved, he jerked awake, looking just as disoriented as she had felt.

She got up and shut off her alarm, then picked up his phone and handed it to him as he blinked and seemed to figure out where he was.

Thankfully the two hours of sleep, while not leaving her feeling completely refreshed, at least made her feel like she could stay awake for the drive to Fargo.

He shut his alarm off, and she said immediately, "I'm sorry. I didn't realize that I had moved over in my sleep."

"Looks like I did too," he said, his voice still groggy and rough with sleep.

"I can do this myself. I've driven to Fargo plenty of times, and I'll be fine. You go ahead and go back to bed."

They had actually talked about him riding with her, but she didn't want him to. She needed time to think. Time to be alone. Time to process the idea that this stranger, this man she barely knew, would be her husband.

Her husband.

It wasn't just about making promises, it was about all the married things.

"I can go."

"No. I insist. In fact, I would prefer to go by myself." That was rude. She knew it as the words were coming out of her mouth, but she didn't know how to say it. She wanted to be alone. She needed to be alone.

"Oh. Okay."

Thankfully he didn't argue. She let out the breath she didn't know she had been holding, and almost thanked him, but figured that would be ridiculous. Thank him for not going? She didn't want to insult him even more.

When she got home, she would apologize for being rude. Maybe she could blame it on just waking up, although, if she were going to be completely honest, she would blame it on waking up in his arms. Or what constituted his arms.

"I should be back by nine."

"All right."

She walked out of the living room, not giving him a chance to say anything more. She didn't want him to ask any questions or demand the answers she wasn't sure she could give.

Chapter 23

S mith shoved the hammer in his pocket and picked up the portable drill.

He had fixed all the things he could find in the low rowhouse that had needed it, and now he was pretty confident that it was as sturdy as it could possibly be.

He cleaned up some of the scattered tools they had left behind as they hurried into the house that morning to take a nap.

He hadn't gone back to bed when Abrielle had left.

He waited for her to go, confused, since he'd thought they were getting along really well, but she seemed in a big hurry to get away from him.

He probably owed her another apology.

He hadn't meant to move over on the couch or end up kind of, sort of, holding her.

He supposed it was a little chilly in the room, and he had been moving toward her heat without knowing it, but he didn't remember anything.

She'd obviously thought he was trying to take advantage of her. He hadn't been, but that probably meant she had changed her mind completely about the whole marriage thing. If she couldn't trust him to stay on his end of the couch two days after they met, she wouldn't want to be married to him.

Pressing his lips together, he smacked his leg with his hand, just out of frustration.

No wonder she ran off without him. He would have scared himself if he had done that to himself.

Pulling out his phone, he saw that it was almost ten.

She had said she'd be back at nine.

He wasn't supposed to worry about her. He was sure of that much anyway. After all, he'd only known her for a few days.

Not even long enough to get her phone number so he could call her and find out if she was okay.

He should have insisted on going.

Taking the tools back into the shed, he looked around again. He'd gotten a quick glance around it when he'd come out that morning. But it had been dark. And he had been working steadily since then.

She had left without eating, so he had decided he wasn't going to eat anything until she got back.

Maybe she was stopping for something and he was depriving himself unnecessarily, but he couldn't stand the idea that she had worked as hard as he had, and he was eating when she wasn't.

That wasn't right, and it wasn't something that a real man should do. In his eyes anyway. He couldn't expect her to work beside him, under worse conditions, doing the same amount of work.

He had been brought up that women were supposed to be protected, cared for, that a man was supposed to provide. That was the biblical command. And it didn't mean that women couldn't work, it just meant that men had to. And physically, women were more slender and delicate as a general rule and the man was supposed to take the brunt of the hard things.

He wouldn't be doing that if he fed himself and she didn't eat.

Frustrated that he hadn't been able to do what he felt he should have, he at first didn't realize what he was looking at as he stood in the doorway of the shed, hands on hips, castigating himself yet again for letting her go and not making her take him with her.

But gradually, his mind wrapped around the fact that he was staring at a stack of lumber.

Packed nicely beside it was clear plastic, the kind that was over the low rowhouse for the lettuce.

He saw metal ribs leaning against the back wall.

Had she wanted to make another rowhouse and just hadn't had time? Or...she had said she was doing as much as one person could. Maybe she knew one person wasn't going to be able to handle the work of two, and so she hadn't built the second one.

Walking over to the stack of lumber, he looked at it, trying to gauge how much was there and estimating in his mind how big of a house it would make.

He could be wrong, but he thought it would make the same size that she already had.

Grabbing his phone, he googled them, looking for a video that would show him how to build one.

If Abrielle had said how she had made the first one, he didn't recall hearing it. But when she got home, they could talk about making the second. Perhaps if she got the contract for the lettuce, it wouldn't be too late to plant some more. He didn't know how long it took to grow, but he did know that further back in the first rowhouse, she had younger plants coming in.

He didn't know how long he'd stared at his phone, trying not to think about the worry that ate at the back of his mind, until he finally heard a rumble and looked up to see the box truck rumbling up the drive.

There was a part of him that wanted to shove his phone back in his pocket and go running to her. But he didn't. Standing where he was, he watched her pull up and park beside the shed where the truck had been parked last night when she got in.

He probably should have continued to stay where he was. After all, she had been obviously upset at him when she left, and he had done nothing to extinguish her ire the entire time she was gone, so in his experience, she would still be angry.

Still, he walked around the truck.

She was climbing out, and when she saw him, she smiled.

It was a tired smile, one that didn't erase the pinched look on her face and the sag of her shoulders. Her entire body said she was exhausted, but the smile was genuine. It surprised him.

"I thought you were mad at me."

He didn't greet her, didn't ask how her trip was, didn't ask if she had gotten the lettuce unloaded okay. He couldn't believe those were the first words out of his mouth, but he couldn't take them back and truly didn't want to.

He wanted to know that everything was okay between them. And he didn't examine that too much, because... How could it matter? When he'd only known her such a short time.

She stood in front of him, her face contrite. "I'm sorry. I'm not mad. I wasn't. I... I was embarrassed that I somehow left my side of the couch and ended up on yours, all snuggled up to you. I... I also panicked a little, because I guess that made this whole marriage thing real. That...that would be what we would be expected to do, and it scared me. I'm sorry I ran out."

His mouth dropped. He completely read the whole entire situation all wrong.

"I thought you left so fast because you were angry that I had ended up holding you, and honestly, I don't remember moving at all after I laid my head back on the couch. I didn't mean—"

"No. I wasn't angry at you. I guess I didn't mean to move any more than you did. I was just...surprised. Baffled. And... It wasn't unpleasant."

She added that last bit and made him smile. She hadn't meant to say it, he was almost sure. But she was still sleep deprived and maybe talking a little more than she'd meant to.

"I agree. About that last. It wasn't unpleasant."

There. He could meet her halfway with that. Because it was true.

She blinked, then her cheeks grew red.

It was cute. He looked at them for a bit.

Then he kinda shook himself. "Did you eat?"

"No. I went as quickly as I could, got unloaded as fast as they would let me. But I had to wait for ninety minutes until they had a lumper available. It's one of those places where you can't unload yourself."

He jerked his head. He had no idea what she was talking about, but he assumed a lumper meant some kind of person who unloaded the truck.

"I wondered. Worried. Wanted your number so I could call you."

She laughed. "I was kicking myself for running out and not getting your number. I couldn't tell you that I wasn't going to be home when I said I was going to be."

"Maybe we can do that now. Or maybe we can go in and I'll warm up some food and we can exchange numbers over breakfast."

"Lunch?"

"It feels like it. Feels like we already have a day in."

"Didn't you go back to sleep?" she asked as she shut the door and then fell into step beside him.

"No. I couldn't do that when you weren't. I was pretty upset that I didn't insist on going with you."

"I'm glad you didn't. I mean, I like being with you, and I would have enjoyed it, but... I think I just needed some time to think. I... I guess the whole marriage thing came to me very clearly this morning the way we woke up, and I hadn't been thinking along those lines at all."

"I guess I hadn't been either. Thinking about wanting the ranch, sharing it, how we were going to divide it. Also, thinking that marriage was a lifetime thing, and I wasn't sure if that was something that you were going to keep your word about."

She smiled, not offended at all that he had said that he wasn't sure whether she was going to lie or not.

Surely she had been wondering the same thing about him.

"I guess marriage is always a risk. I mean, you can't ever know for sure that the person who is pledging his life to you is going to keep his word. Not even if you've dated for years."

"That's true," he agreed, thinking about how he had trusted Kylie and his trust had been misplaced. He thought he knew her, thought he knew that she would do what she said she was going to do. And he'd been wrong. What was he supposed to do? Live the rest of his life never trusting anyone again?

"I guess we just live our lives, and we do the best we can, and we realize we can't police everyone else."

"We want to, don't we? We want to tell them what they can and can't do. The kind of containers they have to drink out of. What kind of car they have to drive. What they're allowed to say, and what they're not allowed to say. It must be a human nature kind of thing, because you get to that point where the government is telling you what to do, and you end up with a dictatorship, where the people's freedoms are taken away because other people want to tell you what to do and dictate your life."

"I never thought of it that way, but you're right. If we let that tendency in ourselves go unchecked, we end up wanting more power and trying to run more and more people's lives."

"And we never stop to think that maybe it's our own life that we should be paying all of our attention to."

They laughed together as they reached the front steps, walking up them before he opened the door and she walked in.

He couldn't believe she wasn't mad at him but found it funny that they had each read the situation completely differently.

"You know, I guess whatever they talk about communication in marriage, today was a prime example for us."

"How so?" she asked as she turned the water on and started washing her hands.

"Both of us read the situation this morning wrong. Or differently I guess. I thought one thing, you thought another, neither of us was right about what the other person was thinking. We lived with those misconceptions all morning, and if we hadn't just had this conversation, we wouldn't have figured out that we were wrong."

"People always say communication in a relationship is important, and I guess you're right. We must be naturals for doing it." She laughed a little as she shut the water off and dried her hands. "Naturals, or we just stumbled into something that worked."

"Well, maybe we should make a note of that and make sure we do it. I suppose there are a lot of disagreements that could be avoided if people just talked to each other."

"I agree."

Of course, he couldn't have avoided what had happened with Kylie if he had just talked to her. That wouldn't have solved anything. But it obviously solved things today.

He washed his hands while he said, "Why don't you sit down? I was going to warm up the chicken chili I made yesterday. Might as well milk that for as many meals as we can get out of it."

"I can't sit down while you keep working. Have you been working the whole time I was gone?" She reached into the refrigerator and brought out the container of chili.

"I told you, I couldn't go back to bed if you hadn't. So yeah. I...couldn't ask because I didn't have your number, but I did some improvements to the low rowhouse. I kind of thought you'd be okay with them."

"Improvements?" She hesitated as she took the lid off the chicken.

"I'll show you when we're done eating."

"All right." She didn't seem upset, so he figured he might as well get it all out of the way.

"I saw that there was some lumber and rolls of clear plastic and some metal ribs in the shed. Were you thinking of making another low rowhouse?"

"I was. The one I ordered came with a big discount if you got two. But I only put one up, because I didn't want to bite off more than I could chew, and you saw that I wasn't the best at putting it up to begin with."

"I think you did pretty good for just one person."

"Teagan helped me some, and Deuce came over one day. But it was mostly me."

"You did just as well as I could have done by myself. But with two of us, I think we can do a pretty good job of getting it up without any trouble."

"Do you think so?" She leaned with a hip on the counter as the microwave hummed behind her.

He finished drying his hands and went to the cupboard to get plates. "I do. I didn't want to start it, because I didn't know where you wanted it, but I figured I would talk to you and see what you said. I've been looking at videos, and it doesn't look hard."

"Really?" She sounded like she didn't believe him.

"Why are you so surprised?"

"I don't know. I guess I'm just so used to doing all of this by myself. It surprises me that you're willing to help."

"If we're doing this together, then we're doing it together."

She was quiet for a bit as the plates clacked down on the table. "I thought you were interested in working cattle and doing crops?"

"Is it going to bother you if I don't do that, or if we put that off for a little bit while we work on the produce?"

She shook her head. "Not at all. I just didn't want to keep you from doing what you thought you wanted to do. I don't want it to be all about me."

"What you're doing is working. You put two years of work into it, and it would be silly of me to push to do something else when what you're doing could pay for the ranch. Eventually, when we have time, or interest, or whatever it takes, we'll talk about expanding into crops and animals."

She stared at him. Almost as though she couldn't believe what he was saying. Finally the microwave beeped behind her. She gave herself a little shake and pulled the food out, grabbing a spoon and stirring it.

After a bit of stirring aimlessly, she turned around. "I'm sorry. I've been working alone so long that it's just hard for me to believe that you're all on board with this. I would love it if we could look into building the rowhouse. I know there were a few more things I needed to get from the hardware store in town, and I have a list of them somewhere out there. I put it under one of the boards, I think, so I wouldn't lose it. We can look at that, make a trip into town, and get started today if you want to."

"I thought we'd take a rest before we did anything else. I don't know about you, but those two hours of sleep this morning weren't nearly enough."

She grinned. "I love that idea. And a shower. A shower and a few hours of sleep would be really wonderful."

She set the bowl of leftover chicken chili on the table, took the glass that he handed her, and sat down in the same seat she sat in the night before.

He asked the Lord to bless their food, and they started eating in silence.

Suddenly he remembered something and set his fork down. "Give me your phone number please. I don't want to go through that again. I... I worried that something happened to you. And I didn't know what to do. But maybe that was part of the reason I got so much done. I was working to keep my mind off the fact that I knew you were tired, and you might have fallen asleep."

She set her spoon down slowly and smiled gently. "If I get a little bit of sleep, I might still be tired but I usually don't fall asleep again. Not for a while anyway. I wouldn't have left if I thought that that was a possibility. I wouldn't want to hurt anyone."

"Good to hear."

They exchanged numbers, and just having her phone number somehow made him feel better.

Maybe he didn't want to admit that he was getting attached to her. Loving the calm, easy way she dealt with the things that happened. Not getting upset, not putting unnecessary drama into her life, but handling things with a peace and joy that clearly showed she lived what she believed.

He hoped she was getting the same vibe from him, even as he knew that his thinking had come around a bit after he met her. The whole situation with Kylie and everything that had gone down had colored his opinions for a while, but just seeing Abrielle and how she handled her life made him realize that he could handle things better. Put them behind him, chalk them up as learning experiences, and not allow them to shape his life for the worse.

Wouldn't it be amazing to spend the rest of his life with someone who made him better?

Chapter 24

Later that afternoon after a good nap and a shower, Abrielle felt almost human as Smith drove her into town.

She had gotten really excited about the rowhouse that he was going to help her put up, and she could hardly wait.

But as she'd been drifting off to sleep, she'd remembered the main reason she hadn't put it up. True, it had been hard to put up with one person, and true, one person would have more work than they could handle with two rowhouses. But the main reason she hadn't attempted it was because she didn't have the money to buy the starter plants to put in it.

She had drifted off thinking that maybe something would work out.

But she'd woken up knowing that she needed to talk to Smith about it. If they were going to have a marriage, if they were going to work together, she couldn't keep things to herself. She had to share them, and they had to come up with a solution together. Or decide not to waste their time on something that wasn't going to be profitable, because they were going to run out of money in the middle of it.

She waited until they were out of the driveway and on the highway before she said, "I remembered after I had taken a shower and was almost asleep that the main reason I didn't put the rowhouse up was because I didn't have the money to buy the starter plants for two houses."

His face didn't react, but she saw his hands tighten on the steering wheel.

He looked thoughtful for a few moments, and then he said, "Thanks for telling me. I...never thought about it. I guess that's just one of those things I don't know."

"Yeah." She mentioned how much she paid for the plants that she had in the first house.

He whistled. "Have you made that back yet?"

"Yes. What we did last night will be profit."

"How did you come up with that amount?"

"I had it in my account. The only expenses I have on the farm are the taxes and the electric bill. And my insurance. Everything else is paid for. Groceries of course. But when you grow produce, you have plenty to eat, if you don't mind eating vegetables."

"Maybe we ought to have a pig and a cow, just so I don't go hungry."

"I wasn't expecting you to become a vegetarian."

"That's a good thing. Because I don't think that is going to happen."

They shared a smile before his eyes went back to the road, and she chewed on her lip.

"I have some money coming, obviously some from the lettuce we sold today. But in my experience, I'll have to bill them, and it'll be at least thirty days before they pay. I have a few things I need to take care of with that, but it should take care of everything outstanding. I'll have a little bit left over but not nearly enough to buy the plants."

He sat quiet for a few minutes, and then he finally said, "Let's think about it. I don't have any cash on hand. So I can't be any help."

He didn't sound bitter about that. Maybe a little bit sad. Like he wished he could take the previous investment he made back. Or maybe he was just thinking about how he'd invested cash before and had been double-crossed.

"I agree. Sometimes things work out if we think about it, pray about it. I have enough money to pay for the things we need in town today. And we won't be completely strapped, because I can buy groceries as well."

"How much of that hay that you have in the barn are you planning on feeding to your cow? Because we could sell some of that."

She laughed. She'd told him that she wanted to take some hay with them—it was in the back of the truck—and feed the Highlander that she had been chasing the day they met.

And yesterday.

"We could. But if you really want to get a steer to raise, that would be nice to have. Plus, I would have to look at the price that hay is going for to be sure, but the last time I checked, what I have in the barn isn't worth much."

"I see." His words were thoughtful, not disappointed. She liked that, that it wasn't a huge upset to him if something he suggested didn't work out.

"But I'm game to try it, if that's what you want."

"No. If you're sure that is not going to work, or at least mostly positive, let's focus our energies on things that will, or at least things that will have a good chance. If we're back up against the wall and have no choice, that might be an option. But it sounds like it would be better off having it in case we do want to have meat. Plus, if the produce takes off, I'm guessing there are probably ways that you can raise meat and sell that at the farmers market as well."

"Actually, that's been in my business plan. Not that I have anything written down, but in the back of my mind, that's something I was thinking about. Having pasture-raised beef and pork to sell along with my vegetables. Possibly pastured eggs as well. Maybe milk. There are all kinds of things. The sky's the limit for whatever you want to do. You're pretty much only constrained by how much work you're willing to do. And how much time you have to do it."

He chuckled, and she laughed along with him. Because it was so true. There were opportunities everywhere for someone who wasn't afraid to work. And for someone who had a little bit of capital to invest. They couldn't grow nearly as fast as she wanted to without the money to invest. But maybe that was good. Because she was learning as she went.

They pulled into the hardware store, and he got the list from the seat between them. She'd given him some cash to cover the parts they needed, since she had somewhere else to be.

"You sure you don't want help feeding that cow of yours? Or at least cornering it somewhere?"

"I know you caught me chasing him twice, but it's only because he's running after that pig. He has some kind of fascination with it, and the pig doesn't seem to like him."

"So you think he has some kind of unrequited love for the pig, and the pig has some kind of odd antagonism toward the cow?" He gave her a look that said that he thought she was pretty much crazy.

"I'm telling you. It's true."

He shook his head. "Maybe I shouldn't tell you this, but the first time we met," he gave her a grin, as they both knew that was only three days ago, "I thought you were that one crazy person that all small towns have. I'm...not so sure that I wasn't right, but at least I know that crazy people need someone to love them, too."

"You've only known me for three days. You couldn't possibly love me."

"Maybe it was love at first sight?"

Her heart turned over a little at the cute way he smiled at her. He had an endearing grin that warmed her the whole way to her toes and back. That was definitely not something she was going to tell him.

She rolled her eyes, knowing he was joking with her. She supposed she was okay joking about it. Maybe people joked about things to make it easier to talk about other things. She didn't know. But she did know sharing laughter felt good. And she appreciated it.

He got out, giving her a small wave as he walked into the hardware store, while she went around the back of the truck and grabbed the pat of hay that she'd set in the back.

There was an empty lot behind the bakery/bookstore, where she'd been putting hay along the side. She carried the pat of hay back there and wasn't exactly surprised to see her cow munching the last little bits that had been left from the last time she put some down.

She wasn't the only one who fed the cow, she was pretty sure. But she'd never caught anyone else doing it.

This time, when she went to set the hay down, she saw that someone else had apparently been feeding the pig as well, since she saw what looked like some potato scraps and a few partially eaten vegetables.

"Hey, fellow," she said, stroking the cow's woolly fur. "You're not going to run from me today?"

The steer lifted his head, maybe to get a better look at Abrielle, but most likely so Abrielle could scratch his ears and neck.

"You must be hungry. That's why you're staying."

The cow bobbed his head up and down, moving with the motion of Abrielle's hands.

"I suppose I should thank you. You gave Smith and me something to laugh about. Twice now. I wonder if you did it on purpose." She was just talking; she didn't really think the cow was leading her to Smith on purpose, but it did seem kind of odd that it had everything to do with her almost plowing into Smith twice.

For some reason, as she stood there, she thought about the Christmas story, the manger, and Jesus being born in a stable.

She didn't really think that God had any special message for her regarding her cow and Smith and the marriage of convenience, but she supposed that it was quite possible that God could speak through a cow.

She no sooner thought that than she remembered the Old Testament story about the prophet and his donkey.

God really did allow that donkey to speak, literally.

"What would you say if you could talk to me?" she asked, knowing that if the cow actually did speak, she'd probably pass out from fear. So, while she asked the question, she didn't really want the cow to talk.

But she supposed sometimes odd things happened, and they pointed a person into doing things that maybe they normally wouldn't consider.

Her mind drifted, which it often did as she scratched the cow; petting animals was soothing and relaxing, and cows in particular for some reason. And she started thinking about the second rowhouse and the money they needed. And she said a short prayer.

Lord, if it's Your will that we put it up, please provide the funds. You know I'll work as hard as I need to, but I want to know that I'm working at exactly what You want me to work at.

After she said her prayer, she felt peace wash over her. Whether it was from stroking the cow, or whether it was because she knew she could totally trust that God would make sure that things worked out the way they were supposed to, she wasn't sure. She just knew that there was no need for her to worry about anything. God would take care of it all.

Chapter 25

S mith was finished at the hardware store and back at the pickup before Abrielle. She was nowhere in sight. He supposed he could go down to the diner or look up Aunt April who was probably at the community center. But he didn't want to.

He knew what he could do to raise the money.

The thing was, he'd put money into something before, and he'd been burned. The person that he trusted had walked away with it all, and while he didn't think Abrielle was the same as Kylie, knew she wasn't, he didn't want to go down that road again.

He didn't want to put his own money into something even though he was pretty sure he could trust Abrielle.

Isn't that selfish?

He didn't need his brain to ask that question to know the answer. He was protecting himself and not thinking about the best thing for the two of them.

He was allowing what happened to him in the past to color this relationship.

She had opened up her home and told him her plans. She trusted him, when he could just as easily walk away and have them both lose everything.

He leaned against his pickup, thinking hard.

Feeling guilty because he wanted to be selfish, when he knew that he needed to open his hands and let things go. After all, he liked to think of things as his, but he didn't have anything that God did not allow him to have, since God was the creator of the world and owner of everything.

Anything that Smith thought he had, it was all just on loan from the Lord. What he spent his money on...it wasn't really his money. It was God's. All God asked for was a tenth back. Yeah, so often even that was too much for Smith, and he spent it all on himself. In fact, most of his life, he'd spent all of his money on himself.

If I do what I'm thinking about doing and give her the money, and she walks off, and I have nothing, I haven't really lost anything, not if I'm giving her something that wasn't mine to begin with.

That sounded reasonable, and while his mind was definitely not on board with what he wanted to do, his heart sighed with peace when he pulled his phone out of his pocket and called Deuce.

Deuce answered on the second ring. "Change your mind?"

"How did you know?" Smith said, grinning.

"I saw your number and hoped you had."

"Yeah. If you want it, it's yours. I'm actually sitting in town and can deliver it today if you want."

"Got the money, and I'll take it off your hands. Drive to my house, and I can use my forklift to take it off."

Smith nodded, knowing Deuce couldn't see him. "Sounds good."

"I'll text you the address."

They said a few more words, with Smith telling him he'd be there in a few minutes, and they hung up.

Far from the dread he expected to feel, he felt lighter. Happy.

Abrielle hadn't been trying to change Aunt April's mind. Hadn't lobbied to keep the ranch. Hadn't tried to double-cross him in any way, even though with all the work she had put into it, it would have been well within her rights to say she was owed at least for the improvements that she had made.

He felt like she was someone he could trust, but even if she wasn't, he was going to step out in faith and ask God to take care of him.

Chapter 26

F riday night, Smith set his hammer down, put his hands on his hips, and stood beside Abrielle as they looked at the second rowhouse they'd just completed.

"That was a little harder than I thought it was going to be," Smith said, thinking back to how easy he'd thought it was going to be after watching the videos online.

"That's funny. It was easier than it was last time. For me anyway." Abrielle's voice held laughter, and while she looked tired, she had been cheerful all week. Even when she was tired, she didn't get grumpy, which Smith felt like was a small miracle. Because the same was not true for him. The more tired he got, the quieter he got, and the more likely he was to be short. Thought he'd made an effort to not be unkind, and he thought he'd been mostly successful.

Abrielle hadn't seemed to mind anyway.

"I think we ought to take the day off tomorrow," Smith murmured, figuring that they needed to talk about it. Something they'd avoided all week. They spent so much time talking about their plans for the farm that the plans for the wedding had totally slipped through the cracks.

Not that there were any plans.

He'd been able to sell his toolbox to Deuce, which had given them plenty of money to buy the starter plants they needed. They'd be arriving Monday.

The distributor had texted and ordered more lettuce, and Abrielle had been able to tell him that they could fill all of his orders for the next three months.

It had been an exciting time, and they talked about what they would be able to take to the farmers market if they did all the work with the lettuce.

Abrielle was full of plans, and her excitement was contagious.

He was pretty sure they were making plans together and that she was thinking they were going to get married. But neither one of them said that.

It was something they needed to talk about.

"Why don't you go on in and I'll finish up here?"

"Is that your way of saying that you want me to have supper on the table when you walk in?"

"Maybe." He grinned. It had been his day to cook, and he put the only thing he knew, the Crockpot Cream Cheese Chicken Chili, in the crockpot this afternoon after lunch.

He needed to go back to Jane on Sunday and have another lesson. The crockpot chicken was delicious, but it was getting old.

"All right. I'll take you up on that," she said with a grin, handed him the tape measure that she had in her hand, and waved before she started toward the house.

He watched her walk away, her stride confident but not arrogant, her hips swaying just a little, and her arms held loosely at her sides. She walked the way she lived. With an ease and grace that said she wasn't worried.

After spending a week with her, he was confident that he was making the best decision. The right decision. He prayed about it, felt peace about what they were going to do. He felt she did too, but he definitely wanted to talk to her about it tonight.

He'd bent over to pick up the tools that were scattered around when his phone rang in his pocket.

It startled him, because he wasn't expecting a call, had been so focused on what they were doing he'd practically forgotten he had a phone.

Pulling it out of his pocket, he saw "law firm" and realized it was his friend who was looking into the situation with Kylie.

Dread balled up in his stomach.

"Hello?"

"Smith. Did I catch you at a bad time?"

"No. I have time. What's up?"

"I talked to Kylie's lawyer and got them to hand over some documents regarding the case. I know you said that you didn't want to pursue it, but it was regarding removing your name from different aspects of the company. When I looked through them, I realized that you could actually have a case against her. I had a little conversation with her lawyer about some of the things I saw. Long story short, about fifteen minutes ago they emailed me with a settlement offer. A good bit of money for you, in return for your signature and agreement not to sue. It's possible, although I have to dig into some more details, but Kylie could be facing jail time. Not just for what she did to you, but she has some other underhanded things going on. Things I know she doesn't want anyone to know about."

"You're saying she'll pay me money if I sign documents and agree not to sue her?"

Interesting that even just a week ago he might have jumped all over this. Wanting to get her back, pay her back, see her get what she deserved. But he didn't feel any of that right now. Although, he couldn't deny he was interested in the money.

He didn't want to see her hurt anyone else, but he had no desire to get into a long, drawn-out court case with her either.

"Yeah." The lawyer named a sum that made Smith's jaw drop.

It was a good bit more than the amount he had invested originally.

With that amount of money, he wouldn't need the ranch. He wouldn't need to get married tomorrow. He could choose his wife the normal way. He didn't have to have a wife he didn't want. He could put money down on a farm if he chose to or start another business.

Or buy a house and get a job.

The possibilities were endless.

"I'll sign." The words were simple, but they meant so much.

"I'll email it over to you. You'll have to take it to a notary. The money is in escrow. As soon as you get back to me, it'll deposit in your account within three business days."

"Minus your fees. You deserve them. I hadn't even asked for this."

"I'm glad to see it coming around. I felt like you got the short end of the stick, and this makes me feel like it worked out just the way it should have."

They talked a little bit more before they hung up.

He was whistling to himself as he picked up the tools. This was such an unexpected blessing. Surprise.

It was pretty amazing the way God worked it out when he let go and just allowed God to have His way. When he gave up all ideas of revenge, and of who deserved what, and just kept living his life the best he could, God saw to it that things worked out the way they should.

He grinned. Abrielle had been right about that when they talked about it, because that's exactly what she said would happen.

He paused. Should he tell her?

He stopped at the shed, his arms full of tools, as he thought about it.

Sure, it had opened up a whole pile of doors for him. Had given him breathing room that he so desperately wanted, but...what about Abrielle?

Chapter 27

Abrielle hummed softly to herself as she set the table, putting the silverware carefully beside each plate. She liked to make the table look pretty and couldn't wait until flowers started blooming so she could have a bouquet in the middle of it.

Pretty things made her enjoy her life and gave a sparkle to her day. They weren't essential, but they just brightened up the dreary room and raised her mood along with it.

Of course, her mood didn't really need to be brightened. Not today. She was excited about the plans they had for the farm and confident that marrying Smith tomorrow was exactly what she was supposed to do.

If she had to be honest with herself, she was actually looking forward to it.

He had been a great guy that week, and she'd talked to a few of his friends, to people who knew him, and they all gave him their highest recommendation. The worst anyone could say about him was that he was a little bitter over what Kylie had done to him, which Abrielle could totally understand. Anyone would be bitter. But he seemed to have let it go anyway.

She admired that. She wasn't sure if she had lost the amount of money that he had, that she would be so casual about it. It was one thing to not allow someone to make you angry, it was a completely other thing to forgive them and walk away without malice when they had stolen so much from a person.

He had explained to her that it wasn't really his, it was God's, and that made sense to her. But it made her see the farm in a whole new light too. It wouldn't really be hers, it was God's. He just made her a steward of what He had given her here on earth. If she didn't use it for His good and glory, then maybe He would take it from her and give to someone who used it the way He wanted them to.

She had to think about that a little bit more, because it went against conventional thinking.

It lined up completely with what the Bible said though.

She didn't believe that God didn't want her to be able to enjoy herself with the things that He had given her. The same way that she might want her child to enjoy themselves with anything that she would give them.

She froze. Her child.

She was getting married tomorrow. They hadn't talked about children. How did Smith feel about that? Was that something they should discuss?

Were children an absolute need for her?

She knew that nothing was an absolute need, beyond honesty, trust, and the knowledge that the man she was married to was following God to the best of his ability.

She didn't expect him to be perfect, and she didn't expect him to not make mistakes or to want everything that she did. The only thing she required was to know that he was sure that whatever he did was in line with God's will.

She was pretty confident about Smith. As confident as she could be, although she was well aware that people could change.

Anyone could. She had no guarantees that Smith would stay the way he was for the rest of his life, any more than he had a guarantee that she would stay the way she was for the rest of her life.

Hopefully they would both work on getting better... But if they didn't, that was just the way life went.

"Hey there," Smith said from the doorway. Startling her.

She put a hand to her chest as she whirled around. "Goodness. I didn't hear you come in."

"Sorry. Didn't mean to startle you."

"It's okay. Supper's all ready." She indicated the table that was set with glasses of ice water at each place.

"I need to talk to you."

He wasn't smiling, and her heart leapt to her throat.

"Right now?" Before they ate? Normally there wasn't much that got between Smith and his food. This must be really important if he wanted to discuss it before supper.

"Yeah."

"Okay." She waited.

"You mind if we go outside?"

It was dark. They had wanted to get the rowhouse finished and had worked until after eight.

But she nodded. "Sure. But you're scaring me."

"Sorry." His word was simple, and he didn't offer any explanation or assurance that everything was okay. Which made her even more concerned.

Lord?

She hated it when her world turned upside down. She wanted things to just go on, even keel, never having the ride be rough. Just working hard and not having the shock of unexpected upsets disrupting her plans.

"Smith. Please don't keep me waiting," she said immediately as she set foot outside before the door even slammed shut.

He turned to face her, shoved his hands in his pockets, and stared right into her eyes. His face was lit up by the light that shone out of the door, but hers must have been in shadow to him. Still, his eyes seemed to know exactly where hers were, and he held her gaze as he spoke.

"I got a call from my friend, my lawyer, just now. Kylie's been engaging in some things that aren't quite legal, and my lawyer got papers that basically prove that she committed a crime in her dealings with me. She's offered me money in order to settle. A good bit of money."

He named a figure, and Abrielle gasped. That was enough to not just do every single thing that they had considered doing with the rowhouse, but they could buy cows. Or equipment if they wanted to farm with crops. She didn't know how much a tractor cost, but it would be a good start for that anyway. There was so much they could do on the farm—

"I told him I would take it."

"That's great!" She smiled, excitement lighting her eyes, but his face was still serious.

"That means we don't have to get married tomorrow."

Her smile froze.

She froze.

Her heart stopped. At least it felt like it. Her lungs seized. She tried not to choke. Since suddenly her throat was dry as her eyes flew across his face. It looked serious, taciturn, and she wasn't sure what that meant.

"Is that what you want?" she managed to ask, in a voice that sounded almost normal.

There was a pause which felt long, drawn out, and so very, very scary.

"No. It's not. But I didn't think it would be right for me to know that we didn't have to and not tell you. You deserve the same choice that I had. Have."

Oh.

Oh. Wow.

"You still want to marry me?" Her words were soft, disbelief lacing them so hard she could hear it.

He nodded. "I do."

Oh.

She didn't know what to say. She couldn't believe it. He had enough money to walk. To allow Miss April to sell the farm out from underneath her while he went and started his life somewhere else. But he didn't want to do that. He wanted to...marry her.

"If... If you don't want to, it's okay. I know I said I wanted to still, but I don't want you to feel pressured that you have to agree with me." He seemed to take a breath. "Just wanted to be clear about that. The work that we did this week was fun for me. You don't owe me anything or have to make decisions based on what I want—"

"No. I'm sorry. I'm quiet because I can't believe that you still want to marry me. You can walk away. You could do anything. Buy a house and get a job. Not have all of this work. Everything we talked about, everything we've discussed, it's all going to take hard, backbreaking, dawn-to-dark work. Like today. We were working from the time we got up in the morning until we go to bed at night. That's what this is going to be. I can't believe you're choosing that."

"I'm choosing you."

Her stomach jumped and twisted. Her throat seemed to close, not even allowing a little bit of air into her lungs. She took shallow breaths, and without thinking about it, her hand went to her chest. Not because it hurt, but because... She couldn't believe it.

"Me?"

He put a hand on her shoulder. It was the first time that he'd deliberately touched her since she'd gotten off the couch early Monday morning.

"I've worked beside you all week. Maybe that's not enough time to fall in love, but that's not the kind of love I want to have for you anyway. I... I adore you. Adore your work ethic, your attitude, the way you walk."

That made her laugh, and he smiled, then his face grew serious again.

"I've... I've been looking forward to tomorrow. I wasn't disappointed when I got the phone call tonight, and I did think of all the things that I could do, but just in a theoretical way. Not in a way that showed that I wanted to. Because I don't. I love the plans we've made. And I know I'm not as invested as you are, but I want to see them through." He paused. "But I have to admit they wouldn't be nearly as exciting to me if I were looking at doing them by myself. Ninety percent of my excitement is the fact that you and I were going to be doing them together."

She couldn't help herself. She smiled. "And the other ten percent?"

"I think I'm gonna like it. I know I am. But when I look at the rest of my life, I want to build a life that we love together. You and me."

The hand on her shoulder moved up around her neck. And whether he was pressuring her neck, or whether they moved of their own accord, she wasn't sure. But she took a step, closing the distance between them as she put her hands on his waist and looked up.

"You scared me."

"Sorry."

"I thought you were going to leave. I can't believe how...devastated that made me feel. I, I didn't realize how much store I put into you and me doing this together. But, I'm just saying, I've had plans for a long time, but the idea of doing them with you made them all so much better. And the idea that you are going to be here. I'm so glad you're going to stay."

"Does that mean you'll marry me tomorrow?"

"This is a proposal?" She tilted her head.

"It's about the most unromantic proposal in the history of mankind, but I guess it could be."

"Maybe I should be proposing to you. But, yes. Yes, I still want to marry you tomorrow. I can't believe that you still want to marry me."

"I do. I... I've been thinking about it a lot." He leaned forward a little, and she lifted her head.

"Me too."

"I've been thinking about kissing you, too. I know that wasn't really part of the bargain, but I hope it's something that we get around to eventually."

"Eventually meaning tonight?"

One side of his mouth turned up in that quirky grin that she loved. The one that looked so endearing and gave her butterflies in her stomach every time. "Right now?"

"I love it when we have the same idea."

"Me, too."

Maybe there were more things to talk about, more things to say, but she didn't care, didn't want to talk as his head lowered, and their lips touched.

Enjoy this preview of *Just a Cowboy's Best Friend*, just for you!

Just a Cowboy's Best Friend

Chapter 1

J une moved slowly through the house, her eyes caught by the wide expanse of beautiful blue sky outside her kitchen window.

She stopped, letting the sight give a smile, both to her face and to her heart.

The silence of her house was almost audible.

It felt empty, abandoned, which gave her a hollow feeling inside as she thought this was the way her house would be all the time as soon as her youngest child graduated from high school.

"Meow."

She startled, then looked down, seeing Garfield walking silently across the dining room floor. He came over to her legs and pressed against them.

"Hey, Garfield," she said, taking a moment to bend down and scoop him up.

"Where's Tom?" she asked, after touching her nose to his and scratching his ears.

She looked around, but Tom was nowhere in sight. He was a little more shy, although certainly he was comfortable with June and typically only hid when her husband, Wayne, came home.

If, by some odd chance, Wayne was in the house, it could be days before June saw Tom.

But today, it was just her, and Tom would have no reason to hide.

The third and last of her three children had stayed overnight at a friend's house, because they were heading off to a rodeo early this morning.

When she was a young mom and wife, she used to dream of the day where she and Wayne would have the house to themselves on a Saturday morning.

They'd lie in bed and snuggle. Talk and laugh. Get up and watch the sunrise together, go out for breakfast, or just hang around the house enjoying each other's company.

They had been schoolgirl dreams, because nothing in her marriage had ever panned out the way she'd dreamed.

Wayne had never been interested in doing anything with the family or her. He'd gone to recitals and pageants and even church on occasion, when she begged and pleaded and prodded, sometimes even crying, although she had never used her tears as an instrument against him. Sometimes she just couldn't help herself.

She'd been lonely her whole marriage.

But she'd put on a brave front for the children.

But now, with just three years left for her youngest to be at home, she was looking at a life that stretched out before her, filled with good deeds, her work which she loved, and always looking to help others.

But still empty, alone, with no lifetime companion, even though she was officially married.

The longing hit her harder at some times than others. This morning had been hard. Just because of all the dreams that lay buried in dust. And because it would have been nice to have a companion on a Saturday morning.

She would be going to the community center to sit with her friends Helen and Miss April as Miss April shared wisdom from her almost fifty years of marriage.

Giving Garfield one last pat and looking around again for Tom, but not seeing him, she set Garfield down and made her way to the door.

Gathering her crafting bag and the things she had set out, she picked up the garbage that she had set by the door, which Wayne had walked by this morning on his way out to do whatever it was he needed to do, and walked out of the house, throwing the garbage in the garbage can by the shed before she got in her car and drove the short distance into Sweet Water.

Normally she was a big believer in looking ahead with anticipation and not looking back with regrets, but this morning, she wished so hard that she had made one major different choice in her life.

But while Wayne sometimes yelled at her, always blamed her for everything that went wrong, only talked to her when he didn't have anyone else to talk to or when he wanted her to do something for him, and only spent time with her when he didn't have any of his friends available, he had never cheated, not to her knowledge.

He lied to her a lot and definitely had a double standard. One for him and a higher, impossible one for her.

She wondered at times where she had gone wrong.

No one could say they hadn't been together long enough before they got married, since they'd dated for almost five years.

But the little things that nagged at her then had only gotten worse over time.

Maybe she was too trusting. Maybe he lied to her the whole time they dated, and she had just never noticed.

Pulling into the community center, she parked her car, grabbing her things and deliberately trying to pull her mind from where it had gone.

Wayne had done nothing that gave her a biblical reason to leave the marriage, and she had tried as hard as she could over the years to be the very best wife and mother she could, giving love and kindness and consideration, and getting nothing in return.

Coming here today was not to get advice on how to improve her marriage. She knew from experience that trying to talk to Wayne would only end up in an argument, because no matter how carefully she phrased things, any idea that their marriage might need to be improved was taken as an attack by him.

He was uninterested in seeing a marriage counselor or in hearing how he could be a better husband or father. He didn't think that she or the children should have needs outside of whatever he saw fit to bestow on them.

"Good morning," Miss April said as June stepped through the door, closing it behind her with her foot and shuffling the packages in her hand.

"It's a beautiful day," she said, smiling and meaning it. If she weren't coming here, if she didn't need to talk to Miss April, she would be outside in her garden. It was that kind of day.

But more and more, she'd been thinking about leaving Wayne, even though she knew the only biblical reason for divorce was fornication.

Not neglect, not an abandonment of duty, if the husband didn't love his wife the way Christ loved the church and gave himself for it, the wife was not given permission to leave. Just as the husband was not given permission to leave if the wife didn't submit or obey.

It was up to each partner to keep their end of the marriage.

Still, it was discouraging to think that she would spend the rest of her life being ignored and neglected, unable to find a partner who truly cared about her, while basically being a single woman who did a man's laundry.

If she was going to be single, she didn't want the extra laundry to do.

Knowing that mindset wasn't biblical, she came, maybe not eagerly, to listen to what Miss April said each week, trying to do the right thing, the biblical thing, instead of the thing that she wanted to do.

After all, she wasn't supposed to live her life to make herself happy. She was supposed to live her life to glorify God. And if in order for her to glorify God she had to love someone who was unlovable and stay with them, to serve them and continue to be a blessing to them, even when she got nothing from them in return, that's what she wanted to do.

In theory.

In reality, her heart wanted romance. Or at least a gentle love. A soft touch, a kind word, companionship, kindness, smiles and laughs and family time together.

She swallowed, keeping the bright look on her face, wanting with all her heart to let her life be directed by God and not by her schoolgirl dreams. Even if she was in her early fifties.

"June, I could hardly wait for you to get here. Miss April was talking about the foundation of a marriage being friendship. I wanted her to keep talking, but I didn't want you to miss anything. So, I have been pacing back and forth watching out the window for you to pull in."

"I'm sorry. I thought I would be early. I had the house to myself this morning."

"Your husband already left?" Helen asked, knowing the history, at least some of it, and that her husband typically didn't spend any more time with her than what he absolutely had to.

"Yeah. He always says when you own your own business, you never get a day off."

Not even Sundays. Sometimes he would go to church with her and the kids, but he'd pull his phone out and play on it the entire time the preacher was talking. There was never any chance that he might hear anything that would cause him to look at his own life. Not just because he was playing on his phone, but because Wayne already thought he was perfect, and the idea that someone could say something that might improve him—he would say a person can't improve perfection, laugh, and then live exactly that way. Like he was perfect, and there was no improving perfection.

Miss April came over as June put her things down and gave her a hug. "How are you doing?"

"I'm doing well," June said, and she felt that was the honest answer. She didn't come here to complain about her husband, although she had mentioned a few of the facts.

She came to listen to Miss April, and she didn't want to turn it into a whining session. After all, the Bible said if they bite and devour each other, take heed that they be not consumed one of another.

She didn't want to bite and devour her husband, no matter how unkind he was to her. She did, however, want advice on how to do the best she could. Be the best Christian she could. So that others might see Jesus in her.

Miss April didn't say anything as she pulled back, looking deep into June's eyes. There was compassion in her gaze, as there always was. "We were talking about being best friends before you get married. Or marrying your best friend."

"I think that's a really good idea."

Miss April nodded, helping June unpack the bags that she brought, taking her hot glue gun over to the table and plugging it in. "We're taught that we need to have romantic sparks. Attraction and all the tingly feelings, and those are nice, but marriage is so much more than tingly feelings. You need to like the person you're married to."

June sighed to herself, wondering if that was her husband's problem. Wayne didn't like her.

She had to admit, the longer they were married, the less she liked him. Twenty years ago, when they'd only been married for a decade, he still seemed to try to be a good person. To be someone who cared a little about her, at least.

But it seemed like he totally quit trying in the last decade.

While she had redoubled her efforts.

Although she had to admit in the last year or so, she felt like she had given up.

"It's hard to be friends with someone who doesn't want to be friends with you," she said, hoping her words sounded casual.

Miss April settled herself on her end of the table. "That's a great point. And someone might be your friend now, but they might decide that they don't want to be your friend ten years from now. There's not much you can do about that."

"Like when your spouse wants to leave. There's not much you can do about it. That's not your decision."

"Exactly. It's not." Miss April nodded. "But what is your decision is how you're going to live today. If you still have your spouse with you, are you being kind to them? Are you treating them the way you would want to be treated, no matter how they treat you? Are you looking for ways to bless them? Or are you more interested in looking outside your home to find people to bless?"

"There is nothing wrong with looking outside your home, as long as you're taking care of the people in your home first," June said, although she knew both ladies knew it. She was just saying that maybe as a reminder to herself. A reminder that if she did the best she could for her husband, which mostly consisted of washing his clothes and cleaning his house and raising his kids since he typically wasn't around, then she was free to look outside the house to see other people she could do kind things for.

"I actually had a purpose behind talking about being friends before you get married," Miss April said, with a sheepish look at Helen.

"I knew it!" Helen said, beaming.

Helen was a little bit younger than June, but June was pretty sure she was also in a marriage where she and her husband had, at the very least, drifted apart.

"I hope you're thinking about what I'm thinking about," June said to Miss April with a smile.

Miss April raised her brows. "Matchmaking?"

June nodded slowly, her eyes feeling like they were glowing as she and Miss April exchanged a look.

Ever since Sweet Water's lead matchmaker, Miss Charlene, had gotten married, she hadn't been as involved in matchmaking as she had when she was single.

Helen squealed. "Who?"

Miss April smiled at both women, then she raised her brows. "Best friends?"

That was all she needed to say before June knew exactly who she was talking about.

"Deuce and Teagan," June and Helen said same time.

Miss April nodded. "Exactly."

Just as quickly as her excitement had spiked, June deflated, staring at the glass beads in front of her. "But they really are best friends. I mean, they've been best friends for a decade or more."

"More, for sure," Miss April said, nodding again. "But they are prime candidates for a match. Because they're such good friends. They know each other inside out, and they have that great foundation that is solid and strong and perfect to build a marriage upon."

It was the kind of foundation that June thought she had had, but she realized, looking back, that it was what she wanted, not what she had. She had looked at what she had through rose-colored glasses, trying to make it check all the boxes she wanted, when it really hadn't.

How she wished she would have had someone to tell her that she was going about it all wrong. But she had longed for intimacy and romance, and she hadn't been interested in having a career, as so many other women seemed to want. She wanted to be someone's wife, someone's best friend, someone's lover. The person who kept the house and worked behind the scenes to make everyone happy, doing everything she could to make their lives better in whatever way she could.

"They would be a perfect couple, but how are you going to get them to see that?" June asked.

Miss April grinned, a grin that was sly and competent at the same time. "You're going to help me."

June blinked. "Me?"

She was the last person alive qualified to do any kind of matchmaking. Even when her children asked her for relationship advice, she always said as little as would appease them. What did she know about relationships? Just what didn't work. Just that you couldn't put one hundred percent effort in when another person put zero and think you were going to have something worthwhile.

Or you could put one hundred percent in, but if the person you were married to was not a good person, it felt like casting your pearls before swine, only when you made a vow, you had to keep it. It was a covenant, not something that could be broken just because someone felt like it.

"Yes."

"Are you going to tell us what you're doing?" Helen asked, sounding eager, her hands holding her flowers, but they stilled on the table, and she hadn't even begun to start arranging the wreath she was working on.

"Edgar and I will be married for fifty years in a few months, so we're going to Italy for three weeks."

"Wow!" June exclaimed. "That's fantastic!"

"I've never been, and I can't wait. Edgar is not quite as eager, but he loves me and knows I've wanted to go my entire life and haven't been able to, so he's doing it for me." Miss April beamed, and June's heart warmed. It was obvious that Miss April adored her husband, and if Edgar, who had lived in the West all of his life and was perfectly happy to never set foot out of the state, had agreed to go to Italy, he must be completely infatuated with his wife.

June tried not to compare that to her own marriage where her husband wouldn't even stop at the grocery store to bring a gallon of milk home for her when she had three small children.

It had been years since she'd asked him to do anything for her, because it was just setting herself up for disappointment.

"We've booked our tickets, and we even have a tour set up. I'm going to see Rome, the Coliseum, and dip my toes in the Mediterranean Sea. We also have almost an entire week of doing nothing but relaxing at this amazing villa. It's the trip of a lifetime."

June and Helen exchanged a smiling glance at Miss April's dreamy tone. There was no doubt that this trip was something she was looking forward to in a huge way.

After a bit, June said, "I'm not sure I understand how your trip plays into getting Teagan and Deuce together."

"Oh." Miss April blinked and seemed to bring her mind back down to their level. "I'm sorry. I can't believe I'm getting to go to Italy after all of these years. I get a little carried away about it."

"I hadn't noticed," June said, her voice holding humor and a heavy dose of sarcasm.

Miss April smiled even broader. Then, as though she were adjusting her mind to focus on the subject at hand, her face grew a little more serious. "I need someone to babysit my cats while I'm gone."

"You don't have cats," Helen pointed out immediately.

"I know. That's where you come in. June, I need to borrow your cats."

"...Sure. If this is going to help get Teagan and Deuce together, I know my cats will be all for it."

"I have a parakeet you can borrow," Helen offered.

Miss April laughed a little. "I'll take you up on that,"

"I'm not quite sure I see the connection just yet." June tried not to push, but she was anxious to see how this whole matchmaking thing was going to work. She didn't understand how a trip to Italy, a couple of cats, and a parakeet could end up helping Teagan and Deuce realize that they liked each other for more than friends.

"I'm going to ask Teagan to catsit. And parakeetsit apparently," Miss April added hastily, lifting a brow.

Then, she lowered her voice and told Helen and June exactly how she saw everything playing out.

June had to admit the plan was brilliant.

Pick up your copy of *Just a Cowboy's Best Friend* by Jessie Gussman today!

A Gift from Jessie

View this code through your smart phone camera to be taken to a page where you can download a FREE ebook when you sign up to get updates from Jessie Gussman! Find out why people say, "Jessie's is the only newsletter I open and read" and "You make my day brighter. Love, love, love reading your newsletters. I don't know where you find time to write books. You are so busy living life. A true blessing." and "I know from now on that I can't be drinking my morning coffee while reading your newsletter – I laughed so hard I sprayed it out all over the table!"

Claim your free book from Jessie!

Escape to more faith-filled romance series by Jessie Gussman!

The Complete Sweet Water, North Dakota Reading Order:
Series One: Sweet Water Ranch Western Cowboy Romance (11 book series)
Series Two: Coming Home to North Dakota (12 book series)
Series Three: Flyboys of Sweet Briar Ranch in North Dakota (13 book series)
Series Four: Sweet View Ranch Western Cowboy Romance (10 book series)

Spinoffs and More! Additional Series You'll Love:
Jessie's First Series: Sweet Haven Farm (4 book series)
Small-Town Romance: The Baxter Boys (5 book series)
Bad-Boy Sweet Romance: Richmond Rebels Sweet Romance (3 book series)
Sweet Water Spinoff: Cowboy Crossing (9 book series)
Holiday Romance: Cowboy Mountain Christmas (6 book series)
Small Town Romantic Comedy: Good Grief, Idaho (5 book series)
True Stories from Jessie's Farm: Stories from Jessie Gussman's Newsletter (3 book series)
Reader-Favorite! Sweet Beach Romance: Blueberry Beach (8 book series)
Cowboy Mountain Christmas Spinoff: A Heartland Cowboy Christmas (9 book series)
Blueberry Beach Spinoff: Strawberry Sands (10 book series)

Printed in the USA
CPSIA information can be obtained
at www.ICGtesting.com
LVHW011149230424
778176LV00015B/1061